MEMORY BY PROXY

Beautiful, young Dr. Erica Berger has discovered a way to transplant memory in laboratory rats. To help Steve Austin find abducted diplomat William Henry Cameron, she becomes the first-human subject for her own experiment. She transplants into her own body the brain cells of a murdered member of the gang who kidnapped Cameron. With a dead man's transplanted memories, she will help track down the criminals.

Steve Austin will need all his bionic powers to foil the gang and rescue the hostage safely without surrendering to the biggest ransom demand in history.

Books In This Series

Six Million Dollar Man #1: Wine, Women and Wars
Six Million Dollar Man #2: Solid Gold Kidnapping

Published by
WARNER PAPERBACK LIBRARY

SIX MILLION DOLLAR MAN

#2

Solid Gold Kidnapping

A novel by
Evan Richards
**Based on the Universal Television Series
Created by Martin Caidin—Adapted from the episode
written by Larry Alexander and Michael Gleason.**

**WARNER
PAPERBACK
LIBRARY**

A Warner Communications Company

WARNER PAPERBACK LIBRARY EDITION
First Printing: May, 1975

Cover illustration by John Mello

Warner Paperback Library is a division of Warner Books, Inc.,
75 Rockefeller Plaza, New York, N.Y. 10019.

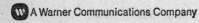 A Warner Communications Company

Printed in the United States of America

Solid Gold
Kidnapping

CHAPTER ONE

Austin felt the whole damned country was beyond logic. The same people who devised tequila could not even find drinkable water. The same people who could do marvelous things in archaeology could not even build a road correctly. There he was, driving down a perfectly marvelous two-lane macadam road built through the steamy Yucatán jungle for the sole purpose of reaching the newly found archaeological digs at Kobá, only to find that the road ended four miles short of its target. It just stopped, right in the middle of the Mexican forest. Whether the Mexicans ran out of money or interest Austin could not figure. All that was important was that he would have to run.

He pulled the jeep off the road and shut down the engine. He slipped the key into his pocket and hoisted a backpack full of equipment onto his shoulders. The macadam ended abruptly, replaced by a thin, crude roadway made of stone blocks. The jeep could traverse it, but it would be better for Austin to approach the site on foot. He could run faster than the jeep anyway. With easy, ten-foot strides he jogged along the stone road toward Kobá.

Kobá was yet another indication of the lack of logic which has permeated the history of Mexico,

Austin thought. The Mayas, who built their two hundred acres of homes, plazas, temples, and pyramids nearly two millenia ago, were the most civilized yet most enigmatic of pre-Columbian peoples. They built great cities, then abandoned them for no apparent reason. They developed a system of calculation capable to determining to the exact day the correct position of sun, moon, and planets, yet they were incapable of weighing a sack of corn. They could count in the millions, and developed a calendar as accurate as the one in use today, but failed to grasp the principle of the wheel. They built pyramids several hundred feet high and a third of a block square at the base, and did it without using slaves or metal tools. Then, for no apparent reason, they built another pyramid right on top of it, leaving the old one intact but hidden. In short, the Mayas seemed to Austin to have been people exceptionally skilled in the impractical.

Austin slowed to a walk when he reached the crest of a hill. Cautiously he peered over the hill into a small ravine in the center of which stood the great pyramid of Kobá. It was 161 feet high, almost exactly like the one familiar to tourists at Tikal. It stood in the center of a large, rocky area surrounded by low, rolling, rocky hills and the ever-present tropical forest. Into some of these hills the Mayas had dug caves, bolstering them with wooden beams, in which to live. The Mayan city of Kobá, only recently discovered, was as yet unexplored by archaeologists. It was closed to tourists, perhaps due to the abandonment of the road, and the site had yet to be cleared of weeds. Various forms of vegetation grew up the narrow steps of the pyramid, giving the huge structure the appearance of a gigantic green plant.

The Mexican government did not have the money to properly excavate the site, so when a group from a foreign museum generously offered to do it for them, turning over all finds to the museum in Mexico City, the government quickly responded in the affirmative, without checking credentials. Austin smiled wryly as he watched from his vantage point above the ravine. What appeared to be an archaeological expedition was encamped alongside the north base of the pyramid. A group of pith-helmeted Mexicans, all wearing side-arms and carrying automatic rifles, stood guard around a large tent, a supply jeep, and a small cave leading under the pyramid at a sharp angle. Austin slipped off his backpack. He unzipped the top compartment, the larger one, in which he had stored his automatic arsenal. This consisted of explosive charges rigged for detonation by radio signal. There were fifteen four-inch-square boxes, each containing plastic explosive, an electric blasting cap, a battery, and a radio receiver tuned to a specific frequency. When a signal was received on that frequency the charge would explode. There were also several score small, round items. These too were explosives, but of the sort used commonly in Hollywood to simulate bullet holes. When in a movie a bullet is seen to pierce a wall or, for that matter, a forehead, the effect is created by radio detonation of a small, round cap. Austin had with him a large supply of these caps, each of them rigged to a seperate radio frequency. Moving slowly and cautiously, he began to work his way around the edge of the ravine, placing the larger explosive boxes behind strategic boulders.

When he completed his mining of the ravine hills Austin stopped behind an especially large boulder and unzipped the bottom compartment of his backpack. From it he withdrew a sizable radio transmitter equipped with a large circular dial. Especially fabricated by one of Oscar Goldman's Office of Strategic Operations' technicians, it was designed to send radio bursts on specific crystal-controlled frequencies at a rate of one every two seconds. One burst would detonate one of the boxes of plastic explosive Austin had placed around the lip of the ravine. The next burst would detonate one or two of the round caps simulating bullet hits. And so it would go. For a period of two minutes all hell would break loose at the Kobá pyramid. Austin propped the timer-transmitter against the boulder and then activated it. Glancing at his watch, he pulled his pith helmet down over his eyes and began down the slope toward the encampment.

He had precisely fifty-eight seconds before the transmitter would begin giving the impression that the Marines had landed. Austin made for the jeep. It was nearest to the stone road leading from Kobá, and was half in the underbrush. Austin, though hardly Mexican-looking, was dressed in the same summer khakis and, after all, only required that this deception last fifty-eight seconds. It worked. No guards were near the jeep and Austin was easily able to slip behind it and plant the last of the plastic charges next to the gas tank. As he was straightening up there came a distinctly Mexican, very hostile voice:

"Que hace alli?" a guard said.

Without showing his face to the man Austin pointed at the left rear tire.

"La llanta," Austin said, *"esta basiando."*

The guard bent past Austin to inspect the tire. Austin gave him a short chop behind the ear with his bionic hand, then dragged the man into the underbrush. He peered cautiously at the encampment. A half-dozen guards were standing in a knot near the excavation, which gave the impression of being some sort of tunnel dug under one face of the pyramid. Austin checked his watch. Less than twenty seconds remained. He took several handfuls of the round explosive charges and tossed them around the encampment. In so doing, Austin worked close enough to the guards to tell that their attention was being given not to security but to a heated discussion of the reported retirement of Pele, the soccer star.

Inside the large umbrella tent two men were bent

10

over a radio set. Julian Peck was a world-wearied man in his mid-thirties, still muscled but showing the effects of too many martinis and too little exercise. He gave the impression of being better suited to a quick nine holes at the country club than to the hostile surroundings of a Yucatán archaeological dig. The man actually twiddling the dials of the short-wave set was younger, less weary, with the manner of a bantam rooster. Peck despised Roger Ventriss, a feeling Ventriss returned. They were together on this assignment only because they had to be. Peck was Ventriss's superior in the organization, but this assignment was going wrong, and that which disturbed or upset Peck brought unmistakable glee to Ventriss.

"Anything?" Peck asked, pacing the floor of the tent.

"Nothing," Ventriss said smugly.

"We should have heard by now."

"Maybe," Ventriss said, "they're not going to pay."

"You'd like that, wouldn't you, Roger? Then you could go running to the old man with that ingratiating little whine of yours. They'll pay. They always have."

"That was before the latest dollar devaluation," Ventriss said. "Perhaps the Americans feel an ambassador isn't worth a million and a half these days. They could give him a *grand* funeral for a lot less."

"Why haven't they gotten in touch?" Peck said grimly.

"It's an hour past the deadline."

Peck sighed. "Well then, you'd better get to it."

"Of course, *I'll* get to it, Julian. You always were a little . . . shaky . . . when it came to the realities of our business."

"I try to fit the man to the job," Peck said, furious.

Unintimidated, Ventriss checked the load of his gleaming Smith & Wesson stainless steel Chief's Special and turned toward the door of the tent.

Steve Austin consulted his watch. Ten seconds. He

11

took the final handful of round explosive charges and tossed them in the direction of the tent. At the sound, the guards wheeled and pointed their rifles at the foreigner. Austin smiled, walking casually toward them. He pointed toward the tent.

"You fellows know where a man can get a taco around here?" he asked

The sweep second-hand of his watch touched zero, and a hundred yards away a six-foot boulder exploded into a million fragments! Around the tent and all the way along the face of the pyramid to the jeep, the rocky soil was ripped by bulletfire. Babbling incoherently, the guards dove for cover and began firing wildly into the bushes, toward the hills, toward anything that gave the hysterical men the impression of being an attacking force! Peck and Ventriss came tearing from the tent and joined their hired guards on the ground. Ventriss emptied his stainless steel revolver at a likely boulder, only to watch it explode before his eyes! Peck ordered two of his men to run over and use the jeep as a cover, hoping to get a better angle on the enemy. The two men raced across the ground, the fake bullets ripping at their feet. They reached the jeep, only to be consumed in a fireball which sent shards of white-hot metal sailing through the air. All along the rim of the ravine the sound of fire and explosions and great clouds of smoke and dust obscured the horizon.

Forgotten amid this mammoth assault on the kidnappers' sanctuary, Austin slipped quietly into the excavation. The steep slope under the mammoth pyramid was pitch-black. Austin closed both eyes, then slowly opened his left, allowing the photomultiplier built into the artificial left eyeball to make the phony excavation clear to him, bathed in an odd, green light. As he worked his way down the tunnel the sound of gunfire faded, then finally stopped. Austin consulted his watch. The two-minute automatic assault was over. He hurried down the tunnel. At the end

12

was a small, boxy room lighted with an old Coleman lamp. Against the far wall there sat a man in his fifties, his left arm chained to the wall. The man had an aristocratic look despite the several days' dirt caked on his usually immaculate evening clothes.

"Ambassador Scott, I presume," Austin said.

The man looked up.

"Who are you?" he asked.

"Austin," he said. "Steve Austin."

"What are you doing here?"

"I came to take you home?"

"Where are the others?"

"I'm afraid you're stuck with me, sir."

"They sent *one man*?"

"Well, things are a little tight. Budget cuts . . . inflation." Austin stepped quickly to the older man's side. He took the chain in his left hand and ripped it from the wall. Scott stared at him wordlessly. Austin then moved to the part of the crypt where it joined the tunnel. He felt along the top of the tunnel entrance until he located a rocky ledge.

Outside, the firing had stopped and the dust was clearing.

"*No disparan mas!*" Peck shouted.

The firing stopped.

"Where are they?" Peck yelled incredulously.

"Mr. Peck," a guard called.

"What?"

"The American . . ."

"What American?"

"There was an American. Right here. He walked up just before the shooting started."

"The prisoner," Peck yelled. "He's after the prisoner!"

The men raced for the tunnel entrance. Austin could hear them stumbling down the steep, dark passage.

"Well, Mr. Austin?" Ambassador Scott asked.

Austin pulled down hard on the rocky ledge. With

13

a great roar, a five-foot-long section of tunnel roof collapsed, filling the tunnel with rubble from ceiling to roof!

"It's okay," Peck said. "They're trapped in there. Get some lights and some dynamite."

"There are a lot of things I don't understand," Ambassador Scott said.

"It's good you're a diplomat, sir," Austin replied. "With statements like that you'd never make a politician."

"I realize I'm a holdover from the previous administration, but . . . why didn't they pay the ransom?"

"Our government doesn't like doing business with terrorists."

"So they sent someone in to die with me. How considerate."

"Please, sir," Austin said, running his hands over one wall of the crypt. "I'm trying to find something."

Outside the rubble with which Austin had blocked the passage Peck was trying to maintain his composure while a handful of bustling Mexicans worked to set up dynamite, blasting caps, and fuses.

"So there's only one man," Ventriss said smugly.

"There must be others around. No one would be stupid enough to send in one man against us."

"Might be embarrassing if they did . . . and he succeeded."

"He won't. One way in, one way out."

"Unless," Ventriss said, "our visitor knows something we don't."

"I can't find it," Austin said.

"What?"

"The door. I thought there would be a door. The Mayas always built these pyramids in layers. They got tired of the first, so they built a second on top of it."

"So?"

"They left a space in between. Two or three feet."

14

"Congratulations on your knowledge of Mayan ritual, Mr. Austin, but I must ask a question."

"Go right ahead."

"What the hell do we do now?"

"The best we can," Austin said. "Mr. Ambassador, I am about to take it upon myself to raise your security clearance to level six." With that, Austin cocked his fist and drove it through the east wall of the crypt.

Scott watched with rapt fascination as Austin withdrew a brick four inches thick.

"Built these things to last, didn't they?" Austin said. Moving quickly, he tore open a hole three feet wide. The light from the Coleman lamp clearly marked the crawl space beyond it.

"Take the lamp and let's go," Austin said, helping Scott to his feet and pulling him through the hole.

"Mr. Austin, how did you do that?"

"The armed forces builds men," Austin said.

The crawl space extended clear up the face of the original pyramid. There was, in fact, the entire original pyramid in perfect condition just three feet beneath the one which someday—if the Mexicans ever finished the road—would present its weed-overgrown facade to the public. Austin and Scott made their way slowly up the face of the pyramid, hampered by the need to move on hands and feet and by the extremely small steps.

"Why did they make these steps so small?" Scott asked.

"One theory is that it forced the priests to ascend the pyramid by walking diagonally back and forth. A line of priests would then resemble a curling snake."

"And snakes were very important in Mayan ritual. Mr. Austin, you're quite a man. You are the Mr. Austin who went to the moon, aren't you?"

"That's right."

"I thought you had an accident."

"I did. But they put me back together."

15

"And rather well, I would say."

"Well, they made a few . . . improvements."

"I am thankful to them for this. And I shall do my best—if we ever get out of here—to placate the Mexicans for the hole you made in their pyramid."

"If we ever are to get out of here," Austin said, "I suggest we can the talk and keep climbing."

Far behind them, deep in the bowels of the pyramid, a dynamite explosion blew apart the mound of rubble in the passage. Peck and his cohorts poured into the crypt. Peck stared for a second at the hole in the wall.

"Mr. Peck," a Mexican voice called.

"What?"

"There is a helicopter! Over the pyramid."

"Son of a bitch!" Peck yelled, running up the tunnel.

The gunman on the United States Air Force combat helicopter found it difficult to speak, but finally forced the words out.

"Did you see that?"

"What?" the pilot said.

"I swear I just saw a fist come through the top of that thing."

"You're crazy, Sandusky."

"No! Look! It's a guy! It's that guy Austin we're supposed to pick up! My God, he's ripping a hole in that pyramid with his bare hands!"

Suddenly Peck and his men poured out of the tunnel far below and began to empty their rifles at the copter.

"Sandusky!" the pilot yelled. "Nail down those bastards!"

The gunman lay aside his incredulity, hefted a machine gun, and peppered the ground with bullets. The Mexican guards broke and ran for cover. Roger Ventriss ducked back into the tunnel and Julian Peck found refuge behind the remains of the jeep.

The copter descended until a rope ladder dangled within arm's reach of Steve Austin and United States Ambassador to Mexico Arthur Scott. Austin helped Scott up the ladder and into the copter.

"Let's get out of here," he yelled.

Sandusky dropped his weapon and pulled the ambassador into the helicopter. Julian Peck took advantage of that moment to bring the sights of his rifle squarely onto Steve Austin's back. But as he squeezed the trigger the copter descended slightly, and the bullet missed Austin! It missed Austin, but it snapped one strand of the rope ladder. The former astronaut hung precariously as the remains of the ladder whipped violently around in the rotor wash. Reaching desperately, Austin grabbed one of the copter's skids with his bionic hand and let go of the rope ladder.

"I said let's get out of here!" he yelled.

The helicopter lifted straight up and away, quickly departing from rifle range, with Austin hanging by one hand from the skid. Two miles away was the coastline of the Bahia de Campeche. The helicopter set down on the beach long enough for Austin to climb aboard. Then it lifted off, made a slow circle while Austin looked back in appreciation of Mayan wonder, then headed swiftly north toward Phoenix.

"What sort of man can hang on to a helicopter skid like it's a subway strap?" Julian Peck asked.

"It's not me you have to explain it to," Roger Ventriss said.

CHAPTER TWO

Steve Austin used to joke that he was born with his eyes open and staring at the sky. True, for as long as he could remember his most consuming passion was getting off the ground, flying, soaring, leaving behind the shackles of gravity. As soon as he was old enough he took up flying. In college he earned masters' degrees in aerodynamics and astronautical engineering, then added a third one in history. He augmented his studies with a rigorous program of physical fitness, preferring such contact sports as wrestling, judo, and aikido. Austin even went so far as to earn black belts in the latter two arts, and found that the mental discipline given him by those arts was equally as valuable as the physical prowess.

Austin joined the Army to learn helicopter techniques, and flew a gunship in Viet Nam. He was shot down in the middle of a jungle firefight, and was injured enough to be sent back to the United States for recovery. Appalled by the carnage he saw overseas, he transferred to the Air Force, breezed through the cadet programs, and slipped easily into the astronaut training program. After years of hard work he was flying craft like the SR-71, a thin black ship which cruised at two thousand miles per hour, twenty miles above the surface of the earth, right on the edge of space. But the edge was not good enough.

As the days of the Apollo program drew to a conclusion Austin found himself the backup pilot for *Apollo 17*, which was to be the final manned lunar flight. Budget cutbacks had forced the cancellation of *Apollos 18* and *19*, but in a curious way this made *Apollo 17* the most interesting and scientifically valuable of all the Apollo flights. The experiments which had been planned for *17, 18*, and *19* were all crammed into *17*, and so it was, at the risk of sounding cruel, rather fortuitous that two weeks prior to liftoff the mission commander broke his arm in a car crash. He was replaced by Colonel Steve Austin, whose scientific knowledge made him more valuable to the flight than the normal American astronaut. With Austin in charge, *Apollo 17* lifted off at 12:53 A.M. on December 7, 1972.

The liftoff was the most spectacular in the long series of manned space liftoffs. It was the only night launch, which promised enough drama. But more was added when the original launch time was delayed by nearly three hours. The launch was supposed to have been at 9:53 P.M. the night before, but at T minus thirty seconds automatic equipment failed to pressurize the third stage's liquid-oxygen tank. Excess liquid hydrogen from the upper stages was dumped into a holding tank near the pad, with a violent but small flash of fire and an explosion, giving a scare to the hundreds of thousands of spectators lined along the Florida coast on which sits the Kennedy Space Center. The spacecraft was uninjured, and the launch took place normally enough later on, the brilliant orange flame from the rocket's engines washing out all searchlights and illuminating the entire area in the light of day. It was the crowning event of Austin's life up until that point. Four days later, when he became the last man to set foot on the moon, Austin looked back upon the planet of his birth with an almost religious awe. All astronauts who actually made it into space were affected deeply by the experience, and none so much as Austin. The wondrous blue-and-white globe several hundred thousand miles in the distance became precious to him and he was filled with a dedication to it and a determination to fight anything which threatened life upon it. While he stood on the moon, setting up seismological experiments, erecting micrometeoroid detectors, and trying to repair the broken gravity-meter experiment, Austin's wonder at earth's beauty were simply thoughts. They would become more important, even crucial, later on, when through another set of extraordinary circumstances Steve Austin found himself in a position to actually effect the course of life on earth.

After three days of experiments, rock collecting, photography, and riding about in the lunar rover, Austin and his crew closed the hatch on the moon, having spent more time on its surface than any other humans. Following his return to earth Austin made the usual celebrity rounds, plugging the space program, talking to civic groups, and performing on the obligatory talk-show circuit. But his way of life was flight, space flight, and the future of space flight lay, temporarily at least, in the space shuttle program. Austin signed up to test-pilot a monstrous beast called the M3F5, a triangular bullet which was an early prototype of the planned reuseable space shuttle which someday would ferry men and equipment to and from orbiting space stations.

The M3F5 was a nasty creation and almost nobody liked it. It was both plane and rocket, with the accent upon the latter. It had to fly into space like a rocket, but it had to land on dry earth like a plane. There were no wings, and the craft had been experiencing difficulty with the turbulence created when an object goes from one side of the sound barrier to the other.

But Austin had to test it if he was to ever get back into space. So one day he rode that silver dart into space, taking off from the floor of Rogers Dry Lake, in California, attached to the left underwing of a giant B-52. At the proper altitude Austin loosed the craft from its huge tender and pushed it forward and up to the lip of space, enjoying once again the sensation of weightlessness. But upon reentry, upon crossing of that damnable barrier, the M3F5 began a yawing motion which Austin was powerless to check. Colonel Steve Austin, attempting to see the out-of-control ship through its one and only possible landing attempt, slammed into the hard floor of Rogers Dry Lake, turning cartwheels, breaking apart, disintegrating, and nearly dying.

For a time he wished he had died. When he awoke from the mercy that is called shock four days later he was a triple amputee: missing both legs and his left arm. His left eye was gone, the victim of a shearing piece of torn metal, and several ribs were smashed to uselessness. One heart valve was damaged and there was a serious skull fracture. His jaw was smashed and most of his teeth were missing. What had been a most impressive specimen of the human species had been turned into a barely living mass of tissue, mutilated in form and decimated in spirit. But once again luck stepped in to to give Austin an assist.

He was flown to the very secret Bionics Research Laboratory, carved out of the base of a mountain in the Rockies north of Colorado Springs. At that location, the forces of science and government were joined: science, for its newly acquired ability not only to repair Austin but to make him better than he was; government, for the funding required. The science which was to perform this miracle was called bionics.

Bionics was a new science, not even a decade and a half old. The word itself derived from Greek roots meaning "in a manner simulating life." Bionic scientists strove to use living organs as models for mechanical constructions. The fact that the human hand works is adequate proof that a properly constructed mechanical and electronic hand also will work. If it does not work, the failure simply means that the bionic hand was not properly constructed. At the Bionics Research Laboratory, under the eye of Dr. Rudy Wells, perfection was the least that was expected.

Bionics grew to include biology, medicine, cybernetics, information theory, and mechanical and electrical engineering. What they had done in Rudy Wells's laboratories was to feed all the processes, all the movements of the organ to be duplicated into a computer bank. The computer told them how to build a hardware version of that organ. It was not easy, but it could be done. And it was expensive. That is where government stepped in, in the person of one Oscar Goldman.

There was no excuse for a pure research facility to spend millions on one Steve Austin just to prove that it was possible to create a perfect bionic limb. The nation's VA hospitals were already teeming with double and triple amputees. There had to be another reason. Goldman provided it. Austin was not only an astronaut, he was a scientist and athlete and, perhaps most important, a dedicated man. He was the perfect candidate to become the world's first bionic man, the first cyborg. The catch was simple. Rudy Wells would make Austin that cyborg. Austin would then apply his newly acquired abilities to the purposes of Oscar Goldman.

Goldman, a wiry, short, and virtually humorless man, was operating director of the Office of Special Operations, or OSO, an umbrella organization embracing the country's various civilian and military intelligence agencies. OSO had the facade of a red-tape coordinating committee of the sort routinely created in government to give people jobs. In fact, OSO conducted many secret operations, usually handling only those of the highest priority, where assignment to one or another of the intelligence agencies under its aegis might prove inadequate. Goldman was a perfect manager for OSO. A former paratrooper and ranger, he had acquired an extraordinary grasp of weapons' technology and an ability to correlate an enormous quantity of facts from an array of disciplines. He also had quite an ability to manipulate people into positions useful to OSO. As soon as he heard of Austin's crash, Goldman flew to Colorado to begin using that last-mentioned talent. While Austin was still unconscious his fate was sealed. Rudy Wells would make him better than he was. Oscar Goldman would give him the sum of six million dollars with which to do it.

Wells kept Austin unconscious for weeks on end, using an electrosleep process which manipulated the former astronaut's brain waves. This allowed surgery to be performed, but without the risks inherent in long-period conventional anesthesia. Austin's damaged heart valve was replaced by an artificial Hufnagel valve and supporting internal apparatus. His crushed skull was repaired using a plate made of cesium, an alkali metal which not only is especially light and strong but has the curious property of emitting electrons when exposed to light. Thus, it may be used not only for repairing bones but in television cameras, photoelectric cells, and may even be the basis for the long-theorized ion-propulsion systems which many think may someday push one or more astronauts to the brink of the speed of light. In Austin's skull the cesium was surrounded by an artificial, spongy layer to protect the brain. The metal fabrication gave Austin's skull ten times the strength of a normal man's head.

Austin's smashed ribs were removed and replaced with ribs made of vitallium and joined with artificial tendons. The entire ribcage was extra-joined to the breastbone with silastic, a form of silicone rubber. In a fit of ingenuity inspired largely by Oscar Goldman,

Austin's vitallium ribs were laced with fine wires for use as a radio antenna.

His crushed jaw was repaired with a mixture of metal, ceramic, and plastic, and new teeth were fabricated and installed. The left eye was replaced with an artificial eyeball containing a miniature camera. Austin activated it by pressing a contact point hidden beneath the plastiskin which was used to repair the scar caused by the same piece of flying metal which removed his eye. Then, a mere blink snapped a picture. After a while the camera was improved with a filter-and-film arrangement which allowed him to take both normal and infrared pictures simultaneously. Finally, when stunning developments in microcircuitry inspired mainly by the cyborg project allowed it, the camera eye was removed and Austin was given a "real" artificial eye. This contained a tiny photomultiplier tube which viewed a scene through a zoom lens, translated the picture into electrical impulses, and fed the impulses into Austin's optic nerve.

The photomultipier tube was hardly a new idea. It had been used for decades in astronomy, to push the capabilities of optical instruments out nearly to the hypothetical edge of the universe. Infantrymen had long used photomultiplier equipment which allowed them, in effect, to see in the dark. The tiny tube in Austin's left eye magnified the available light by a factor of ten million. In addition, the zoom lens through which the tube functioned allowed Austin to increase the optical magnification by a factor of up to twenty; to "zoom in on" a subject merely by willing it.

All of these things sounded like miracles, but all were overshadowed by the bionic limbs, the two legs and the left arm. To Austin's arm and leg stumps Wells attached bionic bones, making the attachment point doubly strong to allow for the extra power contained in the limbs. Wells connected actual nerves and muscles to bionic nerves and muscles. He fed natural nerve impulses into an array of sensing devices and miniature computers. But natural nerve impulses were far from strong enough to run the complex maze of mechanical equipment. So embedded in Austin's new limbs were miniature nuclear piles. These piles generated heat, which was then applied to a bismuth-silver thermopile, a sandwiching of dissimilar metals which, when heated, produced electric current. The nuclear generators fed the current through the bionic structures which duplicated exactly the actions of natural limbs. Pulleys and cables and motors were built into the limbs, protected by a casing of alloys covered with plastiskin, which duplicated the look and feel of natural skin. Human hairs were embedded in the plastiskin and a unique photochemical dye treatment allowed the artificial skin to tan somewhat when exposed to the sun.

The controlling system which ran the limbs also was a marvel. Austin's arm could break down a wall as easily as it could caress a lover's skin. Wells installed throughout the limbs an elaborate array of sensors which fed back impulses into a miniaturized servomechanism. A servo is a fancy thermostat. A thermostat is set manually to a certain temperature. When the heat in the room falls below that temperature the thermostat detects the error and turns on the heat, correcting the error. If Austin wished to crush a rock or pluck a rose petal, his desire for that certain action was equivalent to setting the thermostat. The sensors detected instantly any deviation from Austin's desire, and reported the error to the servo, which corrected it. This is, of course, precisely what is done automatically by the nerves in a natural arm and by the brain. But that was the glory of bionics. The human body works; hence, a properly constructed bionic body will work also. After months of testing, awkwardness, component malfunctions, adjustment and readjustment, Steve Austin was once again a perfect physical specimen. In fact, he was more than perfect. He could run at speeds better than sixty miles per hour, lift a thousand pounds with the bionic arm, or crash through a concrete wall four inches thick.

He was a perfect physical specimen, but there was the problem of mental adjustment. For Austin, who loved his freedom as much as' he loved his life, his new body was the most despicable form of prison. He was unconscious when the decision to turn him into a cyborg was made. By the time he fully realized what was happening to him it was a *fait accompli*. And by the time he came to believe that this bionic business was really possible, he was a cyborg, and employee of Oscar Goldman. He was no longer a pilot, a flier, an astronaut. He was an intelligence officer, a spy, an electromechanical handyman who was expected to work tirelessly in the service of American intelligence.

At first he was outraged and wanted nothing to do with it. But he was a soldier, an Air Force officer, and a committed, dedicated man. The rage dissipated into indignation, which he expressed to Goldman at every available opportunity. What had been anger over his involuntary conversion to servitude finally disappeared. After all, the only alternative was having the bionic limbs removed and spending the rest of his life, as he described it, as "a basket case." That he could not do, and when finally Austin became accommodated enough to the arrangement to make jokes about it Oscar Goldman knew he had won. Goldman had his cyborg, and all it had cost was six million dollars.

CHAPTER THREE

Margaret Simmons thought she was dreaming. All she had expected was a quiet walk down a deserted section of beach near Cosa Mesta, California, and perhaps the chance to find a few shells. But right ahead of her, over a rise in the sand, was an airplane wing! An airplane wing, sticking straight up out of the sand, as though some hapless pilot had crashed into the beach, burying all but his left wing deep in the sand! She began to run toward it, her well-proportioned body straining against the light fabric of her bikini. She reached the top of the rise and came to an abrupt halt. It was the damnedest thing she'd ever seen.

The airplane wing stuck straight up from between two long, thin boat hulls between which a trampoline had been stretched. A maze of wires and ropes supported the structure, and standing in front of it, inspecting the wing, was a tall, muscular, handsome man wearing a blue bathing suit.

"What the hell is *that*?" Margaret Simmons asked.

"What the hell is what?" Steve Austin said.

"It looks like something that came from outer space."

"Me or the boat?"

"The boat, of course," she said, walking up to

him. "You look human enough." She eyed him appreciatively.

"Looks can be deceiving."

"Is this really a boat? I mean, where's the sail?"

"You're looking at it."

"That's an airplane wing."

"Correction. It *looks* like an airplane wing. It's an airfoil, or, if you will, a solid sail."

"I don't want to seem dumb or anything, but why not have a soft one like everyone else?"

"A soft one? Well, I'll tell you, a soft sail is only an imperfect imitation of an airplane wing anyway. Sailors with soft sails spend all their time trying to get the cloth to hold the proper curve. This has the proper curve built in."

"How did you make that?"

"With a little help from some friends who can make the strangest things."

"I've never seen anything like it!"

"Actually, there are quite a few. This is what you call a class C catamaran. This is number seventy-eight in America, and the seventh made with a wing sail. There's a guy down the beach with one."

"Are you some sort of champion sailor?"

"No. I'm a lousy sailor. I just like wings, that's all. Care for a sail?"

"Sure. What's your name?"

"Steve."

"Margaret."

"Let's go."

With that, Austin stepped between the twin twenty-foot hulls, took the front crosstrut of the boat in his bionic hand, lifted the bow of the 580-pound catamaran, and dragged it thirty feet to the water. The Pacific south of Point Fermin was gorgeous that day, with long, low rollers and a healthy, fifteen-knot breeze.

"Come on," he called to the girl, who was watching him with awe.

Margaret Simmons walked up to the boat and sat down in the middle of the trampoline which served to bridge the two hulls.

"I believe you *are* from outer space," she said.

Austin pushed the craft into the Pacific, hopped aboard, took the tiller, and headed out toward the San Pedro Channel. Soon the two hulls were creasing the water at better than twenty knots, throwing spray wildly to both sides.

Half a world away from Austin's casual endeavors, the 12:27 from Zurich and Lucerne was pulling into the Garé de Lyon, late as usual. While less fortunate passengers climbed stairs and stumbled over suitcases in the humid Parisian night, the chairman strode elegantly from his private car at the end of the train directly into the back of a chauffeured Mercedes limousine. Into the car with him stepped his secretary, a voluptuous, honey-haired woman in her mid-twenties. The chairman was tall and thin, with delicate hands, silver hair, a patrician chin, and a precisely knotted foulard, with which he toyed while the limousine drove up a ramp toward the streets.

It was one in the morning. The Mercedes exited the Garé de Lyon onto the Rue de Chalon, entered the Boulevard Diderot and drove toward the Seine, exiting almost immediately onto the Quai de la Rapee. This took the long, black car in a south-easterly direction along the Seine, into the Bercy district, a twenty-block square of warehouses and freight forwarders jammed between the river and the freight yards attached to the gare.

Soon the Mercedes had left the quai and was driving slowly along the narrow and dank Rue du Port de Bercy, along the Seine docks. Alongside a private pier at the end of Rue Nicolai, a huge, flat barge was tied to an old red tug and the dock. The Mercedes ground to a halt and the driver held open the passenger door.

The chairman, followed by his ever-present female companion, strode quickly across the dock and stepped lightly onto the aft section of the barge, ignoring the stacks of crates which filled most of the barge and were its excuse for traveling on the Seine. He pulled open a hatch door and walked down a flight of stairs, the girl tagging along.

When the chairman entered the conference room a dozen young men who had been seated quietly around a long, rectangular mahogany table immediately rose.

"Gentlemen, please sit," the chairman said, taking his place at the head of the table. "And please accept my apologies for keeping you waiting. The train, as you know, is necessary but undependable."

The meeting resembled that of a subcommittee of the United Nations more than that of a highly organized international group of extortionists. Even the room fitted that description. It was wood paneled, windowless, and nondescript, decorated with several potted plants and a few innocuous oil paintings. A large map of the world, dotted with multicolored pins, took up most of one wall. The men were conservatively dressed and multinational. Each had before him a folder, and each had the somber, businesslike appearance of a young corporate officer.

"I believe that when we last met," the chairman said, "the gentleman from Uganda was giving the summary of his operation."

With that, a young black man sprang to his feet, cleared his throat, and began to take up where he had left off a week before.

"Proceeding on the information received," he said, "the minister of the interior was taken from his home without incident. The kidnapping was attributed to a group of white supremacists . . . very militant, very committed. Acting in the guise of this group, we began negotiations with the government the following morning. At first they flatly refused to discuss the matter. But as the deadline approached they finally agreed to pay the ransom. Public opinion, no doubt."

The young man took a sip of water and checked his notes.

"After expenses," he said, "the operation netted the company one million, two hundred thousand American dollars. One amusing side note—at least, I find it amusing: As soon as the minister was returned the government rounded up most of the white supremacists and fed them to the crocodiles."

"A fine profit combined with a blow for racial equality," the chairman said, smiling. "Excellent, Mr. Djbrine."

"Thank you, Mr. Chairman," the black man said, and sat down.

"Mr. Peck, I believe your report is the next one due, am I not correct?"

Julian Peck rose nervously to his feet. His eyes looked redder than they had appeared in Yucatán and it was quite clear that he had been drinking more than usual.

"Yes, sir," he said, steeling himself. "As you know, we were holding the American ambassador on the Yucatán Peninsula awaiting payment of the ransom. . . ."

Peck stole a surreptitious glance at Roger Ventriss and was furious with the look of bland innocence on the man's face.

"However," Peck sighed, "the Americans decided to attempt a rescue rather than meet our demands."

"From the tone of your voice and the look on your face," the chairman said somberly, "they were successful."

"I'm afraid so."

"And how many men did it take to accomplish this daring mission? A squad? A platoon? A division?"

"As far as we can tell . . . one man."

"One man!"

"Mr. Chairman," Peck said hurriedly, "I realize

33

how incredible this is going to sound. But this man is extraordinary! He broke through a stone wall apparently without using explosives or tools of any kind! *Two* stone walls, in fact! When he escaped with the ambassador he was hanging by one hand from the skid of a helicopter in full flight!"

A skeptical buzz and shuffling of papers rippled through the room and the chairman eyed Peck with barely concealed irritation.

"You're right, Mr. Peck. It does sound incredible . . . to say the least."

"I was there. I saw it. . . ."

"And you are responsible for the failure."

"And now I would like your permission to investigate the value of this man to the company."

The chairman shrugged. "Well, we certainly need something to fill the large gap he left in our profit structure . . . but it will have to wait until Mr. Ventriss's plan is put into operation."

"I wasn't aware Mr. Ventriss *had* a plan," Peck said, staring at his subordinate.

"You were so involved in the Mexican operation," Ventriss said innocently, "I took the liberty of speaking directly with the chairman."

Ventriss rose, leaving Peck to sit in awkward silence.

"I've been working on this project for the past several months," Ventriss said. "And in less than twelve hours the most critical stage will be completed. If successful—and I have no reason to believe it will be otherwise—it should earn the company one billion dollars."

"Who in the world is worth one billion dollars?" Peck asked.

"Calm yourself, Mr. Peck," the chairman said, "we are hearing many incredible things today."

"One of the most important men in the United States," Ventriss said. "The man who knows more about America's military capabilities than anyone else

34

in the world. The President's former advisor on foreign affairs, currently the secretary of state: William Henry Cameron."

Diagonally across Paris, in the Neully-sur-Seine section, the crowd outside the Hôpital Americian spilled off the sidewalk and down the Rue Chauveau to its intersection with the Boulevard de la Saussay. It was early evening, and the police, combined with an assortment of OSO functionaries, fought to keep back spectators, reporters, and photographers alike. The job was a difficult one. When two perfectly matched Cadillac limousines, each flying an American flag from the front fender, pulled up in front of the hospital the job given to the police was turned to bedlam.

The first limousine screeched to a halt and from it burst four OSO agents who immediately formed a flying wedge between the occupants of the second car and the reporters. William Henry Cameron's craggy face was partially hidden by a handkerchief and he was coughing fitfully. When he emerged from the limousine a battery of flashguns exploded and a flurry of questions came from many directions and in many accents.

"How sick are you, Mr. Cameron?" a Germanic voice asked.

"Is it true you've offered your resignation to the President?" a Frenchman asked.

"The disarmament conference resumes in two and a half weeks," an American said. "Will you be well enough to attend?"

Cameron avoided the questions keeping the lower part of his face in his handkerchief as the short but formidable figure of Oscar Goldman propelled him toward the hospital entrance.

"Gentlemen, gentlemen, please!" Goldman shouted. "You'll get a full statement as soon as Secretary Cameron is checked into the hospital."

This failed to placate the reporters, but a phalanx

of police and OSO men blocked any further pursuit of Cameron and Goldman. The pair pushed through the doors to the hospital, picked up a contingent of doctors and nurses, and hurried into an elevator. Mel Bristol, an OSO agent who was rising rapidly in the organization due mainly to his singular dedication and lack of humor, which endeared him to Goldman, pressed the button.

"The entire floor has been vacated," one of the doctors said, "so you will have complete privacy."

Cameron nodded and coughed quietly.

"I will be happy to consult with your personal physician whenever he wishes," the doctor said.

"Thank you, Doctor," Goldman replied politely.

The elevator stopped and its doors opened. The contingent walked down the hall and into a room which had been made ready for an important visitor. After some banter about the accommodations the medical people departed, leaving Goldman and Cameron alone, with Bristol and another OSO man guarding the closed door.

Finally alone, Cameron and Goldman faced one another and simultaneously burst into laughter.

"How was I?" Cameron asked.

"Brilliant! Your performance was rivaled only by Camille."

Cameron removed his overcoat and draped it over a chair.

"You're the one who deserves the congratulations, Oscar. You've made it possible for me to break a cardinal rule of physics by allowing me to be in two places at one time." With a grand flourish he threw his handkerchief into the wastebasket.

"Here in Paris, coughing my lungs out . . . and in Peking, negotiating my heart out."

"Your plane leaves in exactly one hour and forty-three minutes."

"Then I think I will follow my doctor's advice and get some rest. I'll lie down for a few minutes." Cameron stretched out on the bed, looking very pleased with the course of the evening's events.

"I'll go down and throw a bone to the hungry pack," Goldman said.

"Oscar? If everything goes well in Peking, we may truly usher in a new era of peace."

"I hope so, sir."

"Is there anything I can bring back for you?"

Goldman shrugged. "A pair of autographed chopsticks," he said, and left the room.

"Going down to talk to the reporters?" Bristol asked.

Goldman nodded. "No one in or out," he said tersely.

"Right, chief."

Goldman walked to the elevator, pressed the button, and stepped inside. Soon he was on the lobby floor, where a group of newsmen were exchanging gripes and scandal in a variety of languages.

"All right, gentlemen, get your pencils out," Goldman said.

He withdrew a sheet of paper from his jacket's inside pocket and read out loud:

"At nine twenty-seven this evening, William Cameron was admitted to the American Hospital in Paris suffering from a slight case of viral pneumonia. While Mr. Cameron's condition is far from serious, his doctor advised complete bed rest for at least forty-eight hours."

Goldman refolded the paper and stuck it back in his pocket.

"There will be further bulletins as the situation warrants," he said, bracing himself for the expected flood of questions.

Mel Bristol was surprised by the speed with which a foul-up occurred. They had Cameron in the room less than two minutes and already some stupid nurse had stumbled onto the forbidden floor. But she was a pretty thing, pushing a table bearing a heavily bandaged patient with an inverted IV bottle feeding glucose into his veins.

"I think you have the wrong floor," Bristol said.

"Isn't this four?" she asked.

"Three."

"Oh."

She turned back to the elevator but the doors had already closed. Chivalrously, Bristol stepped ahead and pressed the button for her. As he did, the patient emitted a low, guttural moan.

"What happened to him?" Bristol asked.

"Automobile accident."

The patient moaned again, and one arm flailed out, knocking the IV bottle from its stand. Instinctively Bristol grabbed for it. The woman who had posed as a nurse brought a small blackjack down on the back of his head and Bristol collapsed, unconscious, to the floor.

"Mel!" the other OSO agent called, reaching for his gun.

The patient suddenly sat bolt upright and fired from under the sheet! The sharp, sibilant spit of a silenced automatic sounded formidable in the empty hall. The agent doubled over and slipped to the floor.

"What's going on out there?" William Henry Cameron yelled. He rose from the bed and walked to the door. Just as his hand contacted the knob the door burst open and Roger Ventriss strode in, the gun in one hand, peeling the bandages from his head with the other.

Cameron made a desperate dive for the phone, but Ventriss was atop him, pinning him to the bed while the nurse pressed a wet gauze pad to his mouth and nose. Within seconds Cameron was unconscious, encased in bandages, and Ventriss was loading him onto the medical table.

Oscar Goldman was alone in the lobby with several

of his men. The reporters were all gone, and only an occasional nurse walked by. Goldman checked his watch.

"Rear entrance?" he asked.

"I have two men on it," one of the agents said.

"Car?"

"Ready and waiting."

"Airport?"

"Alerted."

"Then all we need is our passenger."

Goldman and his men headed for the elevator but before they could reach for the button the doors swung open. From it emerged a heavily bandaged patient on a table, being escorted by a nurse and a male attendant.

"Getting out, please," the nurse said.

The agents drifted aside and Goldman held the door for the group.

"Thank you," Roger Ventriss said.

Goldman nodded and he and his agents stepped into the car.

Ventriss and his "nurse" wheeled Cameron to the emergency room exit and loaded him into a waiting ambulance. Ventriss handed a sheath of papers to the hospital's emergency room clerk.

"Where is this one going?" the clerk asked.

"To Val-de-Grace," Ventriss said. "We did not know he was military."

Ventriss closed the doors to the ambulance and the vehicle sped off.

"This has been some night," the clerk said to himself. "One comes, one goes. Reporters, photographers, they want to know what I think is going on? What I think is that all Americans are crazy."

Upstairs, on the third floor of the hospital, there was one American who seemed, at the very least crazed. "This is Oscar Goldman," he yelled into the phone in Cameron's empty room. "I want this building sealed off immediately!"

The ambulance pulled quietly to a stop at a far corner of the Heliport de Paris, on the Avenue de la Porte de Sevres, in the Issy district near where the Seine makes its abrupt curve around Billancourt. Roger Ventriss stepped from the driver's seat and unlocked the rear doors. With the help of the woman he lifted the table bearing Cameron from the ambulance to the tarmac and then wheeled it to the side of a French turbine helicopter. There he met two men who took over the job of loading the unconscious diplomat into the chopper. Ventriss looked to the sky and stretched his arms in a languid gesture of victory.

"Congratulations," a voice said from out of the shadows. It was Julian Peck.

Ventriss spun on his heels and stared in shock at Peck.

"What are you doing here?"

"A beautiful operation, Roger," Peck said. "Really smooth. And only one casualty."

"Casualty? Who?"

"You, Roger."

Peck lifted his hand and a sharp blue flame spun from the silencer of his automatic. Peck smiled. The job was enjoyable to him. He fired twice more into Ventriss's corpse. Finally he shoved the automatic into a pocket.

"Fire her up and let's get out of here," he said to the men in the helicopter. The engine started with a roar, the rotors began to turn, and Peck took a final look at the body of the young man he so despised.

"One down," he said, and then, recalling the figure of a man hanging from a skid of a helicopter, whispered, "and one to go."

Steve Austin lay in bed, trying to see how long he could keep two ice cubes spinning around the rim of a glass of scotch. It was brunchtime in California, and Margaret Simmons, nestled under Austin's right arm, was hungry.

"The force that keeps the ice cubes moving away from the center of the glass is called centrifugal force," he said. "The force that tries to pull them toward the center symbolizes gravity. In the circular motion one force cancels out the other, and the motion is referred to as an orbit."

"Do you get up to the moon often?" Margaret asked, distinctly uninterested in the topic.

"I try to get up as often as possible," Austin said.

The girl smiled, began to work her hand down his body, and stopped only when the phone rang. Grumbling, Austin rolled away from her and reached for the receiver.

"It's a wrong number," she said. "I can feel it."

"Then it'll only take a minute."

The girl grabbed his arm and tried to prevent him from taking the phone. "You're a slave to modern technology," she chided.

"You'll never know how much," he smiled, snaking his arm away from her and picking up the phone.

"Hello?"

Austin listened soberly for a moment, then said, "Whatever you say."

"What is it?" the girl asked.

Austin stared pensively toward the far wall, then noticed that in reaching for the phone he had pulled the sheet from her body. He looked at her for a long moment, then sighed deeply and swung his feet to the floor.

"Oh, hell," he said.

CHAPTER FOUR

Sirens wailing, the ambulance spun off the Boulevard de Bourdon onto the Rue Chauveau, past the crowd of reporters and photographers, and into the emergency ramp. Two attendants were on the concrete almost before the ambulance stopped moving, tugging open the rear doors, unloading the blanket-and-bandage-covered body from the vehicle and onto a medical table. They raced through the emergency room, through a pair of automatic doors, down a hall, and into an elevator. Seconds later they were in an operating room, lifting the body from the mobile table to the more permanent operating table. Then they departed without a backward glance.

A single surgical lamp threw a single intense pool of light on the operating table as the body rose to a sitting position and began stripping off its bandages.

"Thanks for coming, Steve," Oscar Goldman said.

"How could I refuse you, Oscar? It's the first time you've ever said please."

"I hope I didn't take you away from anything important."

"I was just laying around."

"Good. This whole matter is quite . . . uh, tricky."

Austin slipped off the last of the bandages and lowered his feet to the floor. He took a long look at Goldman. His superior had lost his usual self-assuredness. He no longer looked the master planner, but rather was a haggard, worried man charged with an awesome responsibility.

"I can see that," Austin said. "But tell me one thing. Why bring me in this way? Why not the front door? I feel like a fugitive from an Egyptian tomb."

"I couldn't very well parade you past those reporters. They're not buying half of what I tell them now. Besides, it's poetic justice. That's how they got Cameron out of here."

"In an ambulance?"

"I even held the door for them," Goldman said ruefully.

"What was Cameron doing here in the first place?"

"It was our cover. He was literally going to sneak out the back door and hop a plane for Peking."

"Whose idea was that?"

"That's not important," Goldman said stiffly.

"I understand."

"The Chinese are furious. It isn't every day they roll out the old man to wait for someone who never shows up."

"What, no more long swims down the Yangtze?"

Goldman took a small manila envelope from his pocket and emptied the contents onto the operating table. Austin inspected a man's ring and a pair of eyeglasses.

"Those were left at our embassy. The President gave Cameron that ring for his fiftieth birthday. As for the glasses, we checked Cameron's optometrist. That's his prescription."

The doors opened and Mel Bristol stuck his head in.

"Chief? Washington's on the line."

"Nobody in particular?" Austin asked. "The whole damn city?"

"Steve Austin—Mel Bristol."

The two men shook hands, then followed Goldman

44

out of the operating room and down the hall to a hospital room which had been turned into a veritable command post.

"I followed you to the moon, Colonel," Bristol said, "on television."

"You probably saw a lot more of it than I did."

"There's one more thing, Steve," Goldman said. "I wish you were sitting down for this, but . . . we can have William Cameron back . . . for one billion dollars . . . in gold."

"Jesus."

"That's even more than you're worth, isn't it," Goldman said.

"No one's worth that," Bristol said, then quickly added, "I mean, balance of payments, trade deficits . . . do we *have* a billion in gold?"

"What's the deadline?" Austin asked.

"Forty-eight hours."

The trio entered the room. The bed was gone, replaced by folding tables, telephones, and agents.

"We were able to justify the phones, claiming Cameron's possible prolonged stay here. Naturally, he has to remain in constant touch with Washington."

"Naturally."

"But those reporters smell something more than a virus in the air," Goldman said, picking up a phone.

"Goldman . . . No, sir, nothing new; we're exploring every contact we have. If it *is* a major power they won't be able to keep it secret for long. . . . Has there been any decision on payment yet? . . . Yes, I'll be in touch as soon as anything develops on this end." Goldman hung up the phone.

"Oscar, you're sweating."

"Are they going to pay?" Bristol asked.

"They haven't decided yet."

"Even if they do, there's no guarantee we'll get Cameron back," Austin said.

"That's exactly the way Washington feels. Almost

45

any country—friendly or otherwise—would like to get their hands on him, and what he knows."

"What's my assignment, Oscar?"

"Officially, you're just one of thousands of men searching for William Cameron."

"And unofficially?"

"You're my billion-to-one shot."

"What's that supposed to mean?"

"Come along and I'll show you."

Austin and Bristol exchanged glances, searching for some clue as to what Goldman had in mind, then began to trail after him.

"I didn't even know you were on the team," Bristol said.

"You might call me the designated hitter," Austin said.

"As you know, Steve," Goldman said, "I was against the Mexican operation. I felt it was too risky for both the ambassador and you. I was delighted to have been proven wrong."

"You want me to get Cameron out before the forty-eight hours are up?"

Goldman paused outside a laboratory door.

"If we do manage to locate him, we can't send in the Marines. One man, one chance, is all we'll have. Just like in Mexico."

"Oscar, I need someplace to start."

"Well, we do have one lead."

Goldman pushed open the door and the three men entered a large, crisp, clean laboratory strikingly like the one in which Rudy Wells had created Austin's bionic parts. At the near end of the room, standing over the body of Roger Ventriss, was Rudy Wells.

"Rudy!"

"Hello, Steve."

"The last time I looked, you were in Washington."

"Yes, explaining why the Bionics Research Laboratory computer was used to figure out the proper airfoil for your damned catamaran."

"A man's got to have his day in the sun, Rudy."

"Well, this one had his." Rudy Wells indicated the body.

"We found him at the Paris Heliport, dressed in a hospital attendant's uniform," Goldman said. "I'm not sure, but I think I remember having seen him in the hospital the night Cameron was taken."

"Who is he?" Austin asked.

"We don't know . . . yet."

"We ran his fingerprints through every computer in the country," Bristol said, "and came up blank."

"Well, when he comes around we can question him."

"I'm afraid he won't be very responsive, Steve. He's dead."

"Some lead."

"Don't give up yet," Rudy Wells said. "I want you to meet someone. Dr. Bergner!"

Dr. Erica Bergner was a young, vibrant woman in her early thirties. She was at the opposite end of the laboratory, working with a large, wooden maze and several cages of experimental rats.

"Dr. Bergner," Wells said, "may I present Colonel Austin and Mr. Bristol."

"I wasn't aware you knew Colonel Austin, Dr. Wells," Dr. Bergner said.

"We're old friends," Austin replied.

"I'm very interested in Rudy's experiments with bionic limbs," she said.

"I have more than a passing interest in them myself."

"Are you a scientist, Colonel Austin? Yes, of course you are. You were—are—an astronaut. As I recall, you were the man who discovered the orange soil on the moon."

"No, that was the other fellow. He was the scientist. I was just the chauffeur."

"You're too modest, Colonel. I would very much like to discuss your work someday."

47

"At the moment," Goldman interrupted, "we're more interested in Dr. Bergner's field."

"What field is that?" Austin asked.

"Rats."

"Would you give Colonel Austin a demonstration?"

"Certainly. Look at the maze. Here we have three rats, identical in every respect but one."

She took the first rat from its cage and set it down at the start of the maze. The rodent ran the course perfectly and was rewarded at the end with a food pellet.

"The first one took eight months to learn this particular maze."

She returned the first rat to its cage and picked up the second one. She set it down at the start of the maze. The rat took off down one corridor and within seconds was hopelessly lost.

"This second one has never seen it before. As you can tell."

She replaced the befuddled animal in its cage and picked up the third rat, stroking it proudly. "This rat," she said, "has never seen the maze either."

She set the animal down at the start. It zipped through the passages with the same alacrity shown by the first one.

"What is he," Bristol asked, "some sort of fast learner or something?"

"It's a she," Dr. Bergner said. "And she has one distinct advantage over the second rat. She was endowed with the first rat's memory."

"Fantastic, isn't it?" Goldman said. "Dr. Bergner actually took brain cells from one rat and injected them into another."

"Of course, it's all terribly experimental," Rudy Wells said. "The transfer hasn't been performed on anything higher than rats."

"Until now," Goldman said.

"Wait a minute," Bristol said, "somebody just blew one by me. Are you saying we're going to take some

48

of our dead friend's brain cells and give them to someone else?"

"Precisely," Dr. Bergner said. "And that person—hopefully—will have some of his memories."

"Including William Cameron's whereabouts," Goldman said.

"Assuming he knew in the first place," Bristol said.

"No, no, this is too fantastic," Austin said. "This is clearly impossible."

"Steve . . ."

"First of all, how do you keep the brain cells alive?"

"Some live for days. . . ."

"How do you know which to extract? How do you perform the extraction? How do you keep them alive in transit? What about the problem of rejection? How are they injected? *Where* are they injected? With what instruments . . ."

"Steve, you of all people should have a little more faith in science," Rudy Wells said.

"It's one thing to build a—"

"Steve!" Goldman said.

"It's another to mess around with the brain."

"We can work with the optic nerve, we can work with the brain," Rudy Wells said.

"Discretion, gentlemen," Goldman said.

"Maybe I can provide a little background," Dr. Bergner said. "My work is an offshoot of the old cloning experiments. Do you know what cloning is?"

"Yes," Austin said.

"Well, I don't," said Bristol.

"Cloning is artificial reproduction. Genetic manipulation. A human cell has forty-six chromosomes which carry all the genetic information needed to build the human body with all its unique characteristics. The sex cells of a human each have twenty-three chromosomes. So when conception occurs, the twenty-three from the sperm and the twenty-three from the female

49

egg combine to make a full compliment of forty-six, and, hence, a human being."

"During the early 1960s," Austin said, "it was discovered that you could bypass the sexual process by taking a nucleus from a body cell, such as from the skin of the arm, and implanting it in an egg cell from which the nucleus had been removed. That gives you a full complement of forty-six chromosomes without going through conception. The cloned egg is then returned to the uterus, where it grows into a new individual."

"Correction, Colonel. Not a *new* individual. An *exact duplicate* of the individual from which the body cell was taken. An *exact* duplicate. After all, it's his chromosomes."

"I think this was done with carrots and toads," Austin said.

"Carrots and frogs. Frogs have especially large egg cells. With humans it was more difficult. The egg cells are tiny. The body cells are tiny. The whole process has proven most difficult. But advances in microsurgery . . ."

"The same advances which allow bionic nerves to be connected to natural nerves," Rudy Wells added.

". . . have made human cloning more of a reality. So, we are almost at the point where we can produce an exact duplicate of a human being. Or will be at that point in twenty years. My work is related. It is, if anything, a bit less difficult. I don't have to rely on the development of new micropipettes and that sort of tiny instrument. Body and sex nuclei more or less just sit there. Brain cells conduct their work with characteristic chemical and electrical messages which can be detected with sensitive instruments."

"Anything that can be detected can be analyzed," Dr. Wells said.

"I think I hear somebody playing my song," Austin said.

"I beg your pardon?" Dr. Bergner said.

"My song," Austin repeated. "It goes like this: The fact that a living organ works is perfect proof to a bionic scientist that a properly constructed bionic version of that organ will also work."

"Steve and Rudy have had a lot of highly theoretical arguments about Rudy's work in bionics," Goldman said, glaring at Austin for his near breach of security.

"So you're telling me the same thing," Austin said. "The brain is there. Memory is in it. We can detect the brain functioning, hence we can detect memory functioning. Hence we can learn the tune and teach it to somebody else."

"The means are electrical and chemical and would take at least a year to explain," Dr. Bergner said. "Anyway, the decision has been made. We shall do it with that man over there."

"You wanted a place to start," Goldman said. "I'm offering you one."

"There must be another way."

"Are you merely skeptical, Colonel, or actually repulsed?"

"The colonel is a very high-minded man," Goldman said. "He believes that scientists sometimes tamper too much with the natural order of things."

"The natural order of things is to advance," Dr. Bergner said.

"I try never to confuse motion with progress, Doctor," Austin said. "I think it's dangerous, far-fetched, and uproven."

"That's exactly what they said about you, Steve," Wells said.

"Jesus," Goldman breathed. "Why not put an ad in the paper."

"What *are* you talking about?" Dr. Bergner asked.

"Someday, Doctor, if this works out, someday we all shall sit down and have a talk about the march of science."

"Oh, well," Austin sighed, "who's the guinea pig?"

"Me," Erica Bergner said.

51

CHAPTER FIVE

William Henry Cameron took several seconds to realize that the white blur he was staring at was an electric lightbulb protected by wire mesh. Slowly, bracing himself against dizziness, he pulled himself up to a sitting position. He was in a small but comfortably furnished room. Aside from the bed, there was a desk, an easy chair, an artificial plant, and a nondescript oil painting. But there were no windows; no day or night, only the artificial illumination, and the sound of Mozart playing over a wall speaker. Cameron stood up and, swaying slightly, made his way to the door. He tried the knob but it was locked. He tried the light switch, but no matter what position he put it in the light remained on. William Henry Cameron sagged against the door. He knew he was a prisoner.

Not far away, a drama of a different sort was being played out in the board room from which Cameron's kidnapping had first been planned. Under the cold, fluorescent light Julian Peck and the chairman faced each other across the long expanse of the otherwise-deserted conference table. In a corner near the chairman, the secretary took notes.

"Roger's death is a tragic loss," Peck said, his

eyes cast downward. "Not only to the company but to me personally. We were very close."

"Well, we must put Roger to rest and press on with the business at hand," the chairman said. "I will personally supervise the Cameron negotiations . . . and you will continue to search for the identity of your Mexican antagonist."

"I've already identified him."

"Really? You are redeeming yourself admirably, Mr. Peck. First saving Roger's mission, then so quickly identifying this remarkable man you told me about. What is his name?"

"Austin, sir, Steve Austin."

"To use a peculiarly American expression, that rings a bell."

"He is an astronaut. He went to the moon." Peck slid a folder down the length of the table to the chairman. From it, the silver-haired man extracted a newspaper clipping. It was a photograph from a Mexico City daily, showing Austin waving to an enthusiastic crowd of well-wishers.

"Steve Austin . . ." the chairman mused.

"He *was* an astronaut, I should say," he continued. "Our informants say that he is attached to NASA in an advisory capacity. He gives speeches, entertains congressmen, tries to have NASA's budget increased. But our informants tell us other things. He suffered a very devastating accident. It is rumored that he was severely injured . . . perhaps even lost one or more limbs. Yet he can now break through a stone wall four inches thick.

"And hang from a helicopter in full flight. Yes, you have done very well, Mr. Peck. This man Austin is most interesting indeed. How soon can you deliver him? He might be a valuable piece of merchandise after all."

"As soon as I can locate him. He was placed in California a few days ago, after which he abruptly disappeared."

54

"I'd sincerely hate to see you lose another one, Julian, just as you are starting to do so well."

"I won't, sir."

"Good," the chairman said, rising from the table. "Now, let us have some brandy. One dislikes premature celebrations, but this night I feel very confident."

Dawn broke over Paris, revealing a beautiful summer's day; warm but not so unbearably humid as the previous few days had been. In the lobby of the Hôpital Americain a small group of newsmen sat quietly, sipping coffee and, as newsmen are wont to do, bitching about everything in general and nothing in particular.

Two stories above, in the large laboratory, Austin, Goldman, and Wells peered down at the immobile form of Erica Bergner. Rising from sleep into half consciousness, her eyes flashed back and forth rapidly under her closed eyelids, her brain a kaleidoscope of images. Peck smiling . . . mountains . . . no, not just mountains . . . mountains and lakes . . . Switzerland . . . a young black man speaking . . . a silver-haired man listening . . . Peck smiling . . . a villa . . . the contessa laughing . . . the Mayan ruins . . . a funicular railroad. Her brain reeled with these thoughts, each of which flashed by like subliminal messages on a TV screen. A helicopter . . . Cameron frightened . . . a nurse . . . a river barge . . . the ocean . . . a board room with a map of the world . . . Peck smiling. Suddenly her eyes snapped open and she sat up.

"Well?" Goldman asked.

"It was fantastic!"

"What did you see?" Wells asked.

"Everything!"

"Can you be a little more specific?"

"It was as though I were watching a hundred different movies all running at the same time."

55

"Did you see William Cameron?" Austin asked.

"I'm not sure. I think so."

"Where did they take him?" Goldman asked.

"I don't know. There were just too many images."

She tossed aside the sheet and stepped to the floor.

"I need time to assimilate my new memory," she said. "After all, it took me—him—a lifetime to compile it."

"We don't have a lifetime, Doctor," Goldman said, "we have thirty-two hours and forty-five minutes."

"Can you tell us his name?"

Erica closed her eyes and saw Roger adjusting his tie in a mirror. It was him! It was the dead man from whom she had extracted the memory components! It was not mere hallucination; her technique was working.

"Roger," she said. "Roger Ventriss. V-e-n-t-r-i-s-s."

"Anything else? Where he lived? What he did this past week?"

"It will come eventually."

"Doctor . . ."

"I'm sorry, but that's the reality of it." She walked shakily to the closet to search for her street clothes.

"The gold left Fort Knox three hours ago," Goldman said. "It's moving by military transport. It took *sixty-six* crates to hold it. It should arrive in London sometime this afternoon."

"Then what?" Austin asked.

"We wait for further instructions. But we can't wait on this end. We've got to begin someplace. We'll run the name Roger Ventriss through the computer and see what we get. He's got to have a driver's license, a passport, something on file someplace. At some point he must have paid income taxes, gotten a parking ticket, taken out a loan, had a bank account. If he did, we'll turn him up."

"What should I do in the meantime?" Austin asked.

"Mountains," Erica said.

"I beg your pardon?" Goldman said.

"Mountains! Switzerland! A lake!"

"You have a map here?" Austin said.

"Down the hall in the command room! Let's go!"

The three men and the woman hurried down the hall and into the room where OSO men worked phones, checking out leads. Goldman found a copy of the *London Times Atlas* and opened it to the plate of Switzerland. He handed the book to Erica, then turned to his men.

"Listen, everybody. I think we have a name. Roger Ventriss, spelled V-e-n-t-r-i-s-s. I want every computer bank in France and England alerted, top priority. If that man ever put his name on a piece of paper, I want to know about it."

Austin and the woman were pouring over the map.

"Geneva?" he asked, "Lake Geneva?"

"No."

"Bern?"

"No."

"Neuchâtel?"

"No."

"We're running out of the damn things. Zurich?"

"No."

"Lucerne?"

"That's it!"

"Definitely. He was in Lucerne."

"Oscar!"

"What?"

"It's Lucerne! Roger was in Lucerne!"

"Lucerne," Goldman snapped at one of his agents. Get that to the cops there. All the hotels, you know the route. And alert the Swiss National Security."

Austin and Dr. Bergner were headed out the door.

"Where are you two going?" Goldman snapped.

"To Orly to catch a plane. I assume you'll have one for me by the time I get there."

"It's there already, A Lear jet. You want a pilot or do you prefer to do your own flying?"

"I'll do my own."

"Mel will drive you out and get you on the plane. I'll clear you with French and Swiss border authorities."

"You're a whiz, Oscar."

"Get out of here," Goldman snapped.

"I just thought of something."

"What's that?"

"There's no airfield in Lucerne."

"There's a two thousand-footer eleven miles out," an agent said.

"Not close enough," Goldman said.

"Do the French have a seaplane hidden someplace? Or a turbocopter with pontoons?"

"Tracy, you have the availability list the French military gave us?"

"Sure thing," the agent said.

"Anything like that on it?"

"There's a DR-253 Regente."

"What's that?" Austin asked.

"It's a five seat, single-prop," the agent said. "Top end is a hundred seventy-seven miles an hour. Think you can fly it?"

"I'll have a shot at it," Austin said. "Where is it?"

"Bristol will take you there," Goldman said. "Now get out of here."

Within an hour Austin and Erica were in the air, cruising easily over a low series of pure, white cumulous clouds. Austin occupied the pilot's seat, reveling in the sensation of flight, which had always been his greatest joy. Erica Bergner was in the passenger compartment, changing from her hospital robe to street clothes.

"Need any help?" Austin called, coyly.

"*No*. Besides, you forgot."

"What did I forget?"

"Today I'm Roger."

"Jesus, that's the biggest bringdown since the fall of the Roman Empire."

"Colonel Austin, are you implying that you're attracted to me?"

"Does a bear shit in the woods?"

"Excuse me?"

"Just a little saying we use around NASA. I apologize."

"Oh, that's quite all right," she said, slipping into the seat next to him, dressed in a fashionable, light dress.

"Why did you pick Switzerland?"

"It was the strongest impression. As Oscar said, we have to start someplace."

"Did you volunteer for this duty or were you drafted?" he asked.

"I was the most logical choice. I've been doing research for several years. I know what to expect—within reason—and how to cope with it. I also have . . ."

"Something wrong?"

"Not with *me*. But what were you doing hanging from a helicopter over a Mexican ruin?"

"*What?*"

"I just had a flash of you hanging from a helicopter over some sort of ruins . . . Mayan, perhaps."

"You mean *Roger* saw me?"

"Yes . . . shouldn't he have?"

"Not unless he was a Mexican revolutionary."

"What *were* you doing?"

"The American ambassador to Mexico was kidnapped and held for ransom by a group of Mexican terrorists. At least we *thought* they were Mexican terrorists." Austin wrestled with the implications of Roger Ventriss having been at Kobá.

"And you rescued him?"

"Right."

"By helicopter?"

"I went in on foot. The helicopter picked us up."

59

Suddenly Erica broke in a smile "How *did* you do that?" she asked. "It's been plaguing—it *was* plaguing Roger for days."

"How did I do what?"

"Break the holes in those walls?"

Austin cleared his throat uncomfortably and rose from his seat.

"Hey, where are you going?"

"To get lunch. It's got to be warmed up by now."

"Who's going to fly this thing?"

He patted the top of her head. "Automatic pilot. It flies itself. Everything's automated these days."

Austin slipped into the passenger cabin and returned with two aluminum trays of preprepared food.

"Filet of sole for you," he said. "And steak, medium-rare, for me. Enjoy your lunch."

Austin dug into his food, then noticed Erica staring distastefully at her plate.

"The fish does not please?"

"I detest fish."

"Then why did you ask Mel to get it for you?"

"I don't know. It just slipped out."

"Roger?"

Erica shrugged and set aside the plate.

"Well, at least I don't have a craving for a cigar," she said glumly.

"You're enjoying this, aren't you?" Austin asked, switching plates with her and brushing aside her protests.

"You make it sound immoral," she replied.

"I mean, it's more to you than a way to find William Cameron."

"How did you feel when you first set foot on the moon? You don't have to tell me . . . exhilarated, grateful that you'd made it, awed by your accomplishment, perhaps even frightened by it."

"Right on the last point. I spent a lot of time thinking about how to get back down."

"Perhaps I'll think of that later. But at the moment I'm too busy feeling exhilarated."

"Enjoy it."

"I suppose I *will* tire of being a guinea pig."

"You'll get used to it after a while," Austin said.

Austin took the plane off automatic pilot and, with the appropriate flight-path designations from ground stations, rose over the glorious splendor of the French Alps, across the border, and into Switzerland. Before long Lake Lucerne was laid out before them like a giant diamond in a field of white-capped mountains. Austin dropped to five thousand feet, made a wide circle, and soared between the majestic heights of Mount Pilatus and Mount Stanserhorn. He followed the valley down to the edge of the lake, then made a slow left turn and skimmed to a perfect landing offshore by the National Museum at Tribschen, the one-time home of Richard Wagner.

"Wagner wrote part of *The Ring* in there," Erica said.

"*The Ring?*"

"One of the greatest operas of all time."

"I don't like opera."

"You're kidding?"

"No. I hate opera."

"How can anybody hate opera?"

"In fact, I actually loathe it."

"I just don't understand."

"Well, it's not a *crime*."

"What *do* you like?"

"If you're an opera fanatic, I doubt you would want to know."

"Where shall we land?"

"We *have* landed. The question is: Where is the hotel?"

"Search me."

"That comes later."

"Colonel Austin!"

"I *said* you wouldn't want to know what I like."

Austin steered the plane toward the public beach at Lido and pulled it onto the sand. He helped Erica onto the beach just as a patrolman came running up.

"Colonel Austin?" the guard asked breathlessly.

"That's me."

"We were told when to expect you, but not where to expect you. I am honored."

"And I'm glad to meet you," Austin said. "Can you keep an eye on the plane while I get a cab?"

"Certainly. Is there anything else?"

"Not unless you have a bloody mary in your pocket," Austin said, taking the woman's hand and walking across the beach toward the road.

CHAPTER SIX

Lucerne is half superhighway, half cobblestone lane. Down the street from a tenth-century monastic building is a high-rise hotel with a penthouse restaurant and lobby casino. A few kilometers from a sandy beach is a ski slope. Lucerne is as diverse as Mexico, Austin thought, if a good deal less enigmatic. And it certainly had brave cab drivers.

The cab Austin and Erica Bergner picked up on the Lidostrasse was an old Citroen, painted brown along the sides and orange down the middle and over the top. The driver looked sane enough, but his driving, particularly as superhighway turned into cobblestone, was something else. The old cab weaved and bounced, taking at dizzying speeds one-lane roads barely wide enough for a fat goat.

"This guy makes a kamikaze pilot look like a coward," Austin said. "Slow down, would you, friend!"

"I am driving too fast?" the old man said in broken English.

"Something like that."

"You would like me to slow down?"

"Right."

"Then you would like a tour," the driver said.

"No, no tour. Just the Hotel Schweitzerhof."

"A short tour. Up and down a few hills, I show

you a few sights. So it costs you another dollar or so. All Americans are rich anyway."

"Come on, Steve," Erica said, "maybe—Roger—will spot something."

"All right," Austin said, "but just a few minutes. On the way to the hotel."

"Good," the driver said happily. "Lucerne is a beautiful city. I can tell you about it. It was founded about seven hundred years after the birth of Our Lord, by monks of the Benedictine abbey of St. Leodegar—they built it here. Before then, just fishermen in huts, you know? After the abbey, then more monks, then more fishermen, then the pass to the south in . . . uh . . . the thirteenth century sometime, tradesmen, and marketplaces. The city grows ever since. Now we have maybe seventy-five thousand people, maybe eighty thousand. A lot of people come here each year, like you. Except you are not like them."

"I'm not?"

"No, they stay in the new hotels and look at the old places. You stay in an old hotel, you know . . . and tomorrow I come by and pick you up and take you to look at—"

"The new places."

"No! The old places, like everyone else. You want me to stop so you can buy a fish?" The driver pulled into a narrow street in a hilly area off the Lowenstrasse. On each side were multicolored awnings shading fruit and fish stands.

"Hey, I don't need a fish," Austin said, "now come on."

"Okay, okay."

The cab reluctantly started up the street, and reached the corner when a sleek, black Mercedes slammed to a stop in front of it, blocking its path. The driver swore at the Mercedes in French.

"Back up! Quick!" Austin yelled.

The driver threw the cab into reverse, but another

64

Mercedes was blocking the retreat! The doors of the first car were thrown open and two men, armed with rifles, were at the sides of the cab.

"Out," one of them ordered.

"Go to the hotel," Austin said to Erica, then opened the cab door. He stepped into the street, two rifle barrels at his head.

"You must be from the chamber of commerce," he said.

"Steve!" Erica called. She poked the cab driver. "Can't you do something?"

The old man threw up his hands. "Maybe they are friends," he said.

Erica turned and peered out the back window. Sitting alone in the Mercedes behind the cab was Julian Peck. As he watched Austin being hustled to the front car his face broke into a leering grin.

"Maybe you're the welcome wagon?" Austin speculated.

"Sortez! Move!"

When one man opened the car door Austin seized the opportunity to wheel on the man behind him, driving the gun upward with his bionic arm as he sent the right arm into the man's stomach. The man wavered and bent over, but just as Austin was about to bring the bionic arm into play a rifle butt came down on the back of his head and he fell, stunned, to the ground. The two men dragged him into the back seat of the car and the two Mercedes sped off, the one with Peck behind the wheel squeezing between the cab and an old, clay-brick house to accomplish the feat.

Left alone on the back seat of the Mercedes as it careened through the narrow Swiss streets, Austin fought to clear his head. The men who were his captors were certain enough that he was out for the day; they had their backs to him and were swearing at a bus that suddenly blocked an intersection. Austin drew his knees to his chest, then suddenly straightened them. His feet snapped the door at both hinges simultaneously and the door whirled end-over-end across the street. Austin followed it onto the pavement. He grabbed the handle of the front door and yanked on it, but the handle came off in his hand. Swearing, he grabbed the door at the windowline, wrenched it open, and threw it aside. It clattered to the pavement with a noise heard for blocks.

Austin grabbed hold of the thunderstruck driver and with one motion pulled him from his seat and hurled him against the brick wall of the house nearest the street. He fell in a heap to the ground, his neck snapped.

In the meantime the other man had come from his side of the car, ripped a metal awning pole from a nearby fruit stand, and came at Austin with it. Austin blocked the blow with his bionic arm and the pole bent around his arm as though it were a noodle. The man stared at Austin, amazed, unable to move. Austin knocked him unconscious with a short left jab, then hoisted the inert body over his head. Julian Peck had thrown his car into gear and was coming at him! Austin hurled the body at the car. It crashed through the windshield on the passenger's side, remaining half in and half out of the car. Peck lost control for an instant and the car plowed through the sidewalk display of a market before regaining stability and the street, and roaring off. Austin watched it fade into the distance, the legs and arms of the unconscious and probably dead assailant waving grotesquely from out of the windshield.

Colonel Steve Austin, astronaut, the man who had walked on the moon, strode into the Hotel Schweitzerhof which was patronized by many famous, wealthy, powerful people, looking like a train had run over him. One sleeve hung in shreds from his arm. His casual clothes were sodden with dirt, mud, and sweat. His face was dirty from having been dragged to the car

66

and he was still unshaven from the day before. The silver-haired desk clerk looked upon Austin with ill-disguised horror. Still, Austin walked straight to the desk as though if anything in the world was wrong it was not with him.

"I believe I have a reservation," Austin said.

"You do?" the clerk replied.

"Austin."

"Ah, yes, Mr. Austin . . . your wife checked in earlier."

"My wife?"

"*Mrs.* Austin."

"That would be my wife," Austin said. "How is she?"

"Pardon?"

"We had a slight tiff," he said, indicating his clothes.

"Of course," the clerk said, blinking noticeably.

He took a key from a brass hook and set it on the desk so as to avoid making physical contact with Austin. Austin glanced at the key. "The bridal suite," he noted. "She must be over it."

"Enjoy your stay," the clerk said without enthusiasm.

"It's already been unforgettable," Austin replied.

Austin took the key and walked to the elevator. The clerk watched him without emotion, then turned away, shaking his head in disbelief.

Austin rode the elevator to the sixth floor, walked down a short but majestic hall, and turned the key in a lock. He slipped into the bridal suite, and closed the door behind him.

"Steve!" Erica yelled, rushing to him and grabbing him by the hands.

"Welcome to Switzerland . . . Mrs. Austin."

"Who were those men?"

"I was hoping you could tell me."

"I never saw them before."

"I meant Roger."

She thought for a moment, then shook her head.

67

Austin reached for the phone. "At least we know we're on the right track," he said.

"I telephoned the police. I didn't know what else to do," Erica said.

"I've already spoken to them," Austin replied, "at great length."

"This is Colonel Austin . . . I'd like to place a person-to-person call. Mr. Oscar Goldman, TWA freight terminal two, London Airport."

"Do you think they'll try again?" Erica asked.

"Probably," Austin said, hanging up the phone. "Not the same two guys, of course, unless they come back as doppelgangers."

"Who?"

"Ghosts who take over the bodies of living people."

"I didn't know you had an interest in mythology."

"It's not mythology. It's true. For example, did you know my body is inhabited by a ghost? The ghost of Oscar Goldman."

"But he's still alive."

"You just haven't known him long enough," Austin said, surveying the suite. It was done all in white, from floor to ceiling, white fabric, puffed out here and there with foam inserts. It was all supposed to suggest virginity; to Austin it suggested a psycho ward.

"I wonder how many people leave here snow-blind," he said.

"Our rooms were *floors* apart," she said. "I didn't think you'd want to waste time in the elevator."

"Of course not. If we can't waste eleven minutes getting to an airport, we can't waste thirty seconds in an elevator."

"Why don't you like Oscar Goldman?"

"Oh, I like him. I like him quite a bit. But I also owe him quite a bit, and he never lets me forget it."

"What do you owe him?"

Austin shook his head.

"You never struck me as being a spy," she said.

68

"Oscar just keeps me around to open doors."

"You think this is all a waste of time, don't you?" she said. "No matter how close we are."

"Doctor," Austin said, stripping off his torn jacket and shirt, "you and I are responsible for a man's life. I wish I could say I didn't care how we saved it . . . but I do."

"I'm trying to expand the boundaries of knowledge," she said defensively. "Do you realize what it could mean to the world if a group of scientists had Einstein's memory? Or musicians had the benefit of Chopin's thoughts? What incredible music might be written."

"An old song," Austin said. "Man and superman. You can tear a human being apart like an automobile and completely rebuild it. New heart, new kidneys, arms, legs, eyes. But no matter how many spare parts a man gets, he's still himself, because of his mind. He still thinks the same, reacts the same, feels the same. Then someone comes along and wants to replace that part, too. And when you're all finished, what do you have? A bunch of parts with nothing to hold them together. And what does it prove . . . except that you can do it."

"What do you want to prove, Steve?"

"That I'm more than the sum of my parts," he snapped.

The phone rang and Austin strode from the bedroom to the sitting room to answer it.

"Hello?"

"Steve?" Oscar Goldman asked.

"How are you, Oscar?"

"Frustrated. Do you have any idea how long it takes just to *unload* sixty-six crates. I hope you're making more progress on your end."

"Roger remembers seeing me in Mexico."

"At that party they threw for the ambassador?"

"The same people might be catering this one."

"I'll get Washington on it right away."

"Oscar . . . I'll need an extra fifty thousand francs."

"What for?"

"I promised to make good on a few incidentals."

"What incidentals."

"An awning pole, a fruit stand, and fifty-four pounds of trout."

"Steve, this is the age of diplomacy. Next time, try a little."

"It wasn't entirely my idea."

"What happened?"

"That party in Mexico. It seems there was also one planned for me when I arrived."

"For you? I . . . uh . . . take it you couldn't fit it into your schedule."

"Right. The two gentlemen who invited me just dropped dead when I told them."

"Unfortunate."

"Yeah, and there was a third guy who I didn't get the chance to speak to."

"Anybody I know?"

"I'm not sure. I can't quite place him. But I rather think we should take a hard look at the catering business."

"Definitely."

"Especially since they seem to be taking a hard look at us."

"Let's be careful, Steve. I don't have one billion-to-one shot. Take care of yourself."

"Don't worry. But do me one favor."

"Anything."

"Can't you use your influence in England to have London's airport put in a secure phone?"

Goldman laughed, replaced the receiver on its hook, and stepped from the phone booth. A dozen yards away Mel Bristol was watching as two forklifts rolled by, each carrying a large woden crate marked MADE IN USA.

"That's the last of them," Bristol said as the lifts

70

placed the crates with a pile of others on a railroad flatcar.

"You're clear on the route?" Goldman asked.

"From here to Dover. Then to Le Havre by freighter."

"While we sit on our . . . crates . . . and wait for the next destination. It's like going on a scavenger hunt without any clues."

"Who's going with me?" Bristol asked.

"No one."

"*No one*? You mean it's just me and a billion in gold?"

"We're taking a chance even sending you. If they know we're tracking that gold they won't come near it."

"Chief, with all due respect, have you cleared this with the brass?"

"Bristol, I am the brass."

"I mean the elected boss."

"They're backing me a thousand percent," Goldman said sardonically.

Bristol stared at the huge pile of crates riding on a flatcar in front of him.

"What if somebody steals it?"

"Then you'll have to put in a lot of overtime to pay it back. Here are your papers. You're now an able-bodied seaman licensed to work between Dover and Le Havre, and licensed to work the inland canals on the Continent."

Reluctantly Bristol accepted the sheath of documents.

"Don't be so downcast, Bristol," Goldman said, "you're getting a free tour; at least as far as Le Havre. And there're lots of nice restaurants in Le Havre."

"And lots of cemeteries. All right, I bird-dog the payoff."

"It won't be as easy as it sounds."

"Really," Bristol said dryly.

"You don't just slip a billion in gold into the trunk

71

of your car and drive off without anyone seeing you. My guess is they'll try to make a switch somewhere along the way."

"That's impossible."

"We thought it was impossible to snatch Cameron from that hospital . . . and now we might have to pay for our mistake." Goldman consulted his watch and added, "In approximately forty-eight hours."

"And what if they try to make a switch before the secretary is released? What do I do then?"

"What do you think you do?" Goldman said. "You stop them."

Reluctantly Bristol climbed into the empty boxcar which rode behind the gold. The crates were quite visible to him through a rather large crack in the paneling. Slowly, painfully slowly, one billion dollars in gold began to move across Europe.

It was nearly noon and the Seine along the Rue du Port de Bercy was busy with traffic. It was another hot, humid day, and thermal lines rising from the murky water mingled with the carbon monoxide from barges, tugs, and shallow-draft *Bateaux-Mouches* which cruised by every half hour, loaded with tourists snapping pictures. Beneath the deck of the false barge tied to the pier at the end of the Rue Nicolai the chairman's delicate hands showed white knuckles from anger and frustration.

"You left bodies strewn all over Lucerne," he said, barely able to control his voice. "The Swiss police are now involved. And what do you have to show for it?"

Julian Peck was perspiring heavily. Anxiety showed itself first in beads, then rivers of sweat on his brow, and these now trickled down across the large-pored skin of the entire face. Frequent daubings with a large handkerchief did no good at all.

"I won't attempt to describe what happened," he said, "but Austin is definitely worth pursuing."

"Pursuing?" the chairman shouted. "Pursuing? Perhaps *he* is the pursuer, Julian!"

The chairman rose from his seat and walked slowly along the length of the table rather like an executioner approaching his victim.

"Have you stopped to ask yourself why he suddenly appeared in Lucerne?" the chairman asked.

"He didn't try to keep it secret," Peck said. "The hotel reservation was in his name."

"Then you think it's merely a coincidence that the contessa is there also?"

"He can't know anything about her," Peck said quickly.

"And you're willing to risk a billion dollars to prove it! Julian, I thought I displayed great restraint after the Mexican fiasco, but if anything happens to this project . . . I wouldn't count on my retirement benefits if I were you."

Peck looked down at the table. His handkerchief was as soaked as it would have been had it just been pulled from the Seine.

"I want Colonel Austin out of the way," the chairman said. "Permanently." Without another word he turned and walked from the room, leaving Peck to contemplate the shards of his future.

The chairman, followed by his young secretary, walked down a narrow hall to where a guard was stationed outside a door. The chairman waggled a finger at the door and the guard unlocked it. The chairman and the girl walked into the room.

William Cameron was sitting in a new but cheap armchair of the sort sold in sets in American discount stores. He was playing a solitary game of chess on a small end table in front of him. Mozart still played over the wall speaker. Cameron looked up with cool interest.

"Mr. Cameron," the chairman said. "I have looked forward to meeting you for a long time. I'm sorry it couldn't be under less restrictive circumstances."

73

"How did you know I would be in that hospital?"

"Do you mind if I sit?"

"Please."

The chairman drew another of the armchairs into a position across the chess set from Cameron and sat in it.

"Would you like some champagne?"

"No. You were going to tell me how you knew about the hospital."

"To be precise, Mr. Cameron, I was *not* going to tell you, and I advise you to stop pursuing it. The answer might prove embarrassing."

Cameron stared at the older man for a long second. "The contessa," he said.

"I have always found it intriguing," the chairman said, "that even the most important people feel the need to share their importance. And the contessa is such an appreciative audience."

Cameron rose from his chair, walked to the bed, and sat on it. "I'll have that champagne now," he said. Without being told to, the girl let herself out of the room and went to fetch it. She returned a few minutes later with an ice bucket and a bottle of Dom Perignon.

"It's only a '62," the chairman said, uncorking the bottle. "I hope you don't mind. Supplies have been getting low down here on the docks."

"Not at all," Cameron said, still in a daze.

The chairman poured two glasses and gave one to the girl to take to the distraught secretary of state. He sipped quietly for a moment.

"Outside of politics I've led a very conservative life," he said as though speaking to himself. "I was married to the same woman for thirty-six years."

"Commendable."

"She died two years ago. I was grateful for the contessa's interest."

"One must never be afraid to pursue youth, Mr. Cameron," the chairman said, waving his glass politely in the direction of the girl. "It's what keeps us young."

"How much are you asking for me?"

"One billion in gold."

Cameron looked up and arched an eyebrow.

"Don't be embarrassed to feel flattered, Mr. Cameron. It's quite a tribute to your eminence."

"When will the payment be made?"

"It's on the way now."

"And when it arrives I'll be released?"

The chairman smiled enigmatically and sipped his champagne.

CHAPTER SEVEN

Inside the orange-and-brown taxi Austin was having his second tour of Lucerne. Less than two hours after the near-abduction he found the taxi driver who had brought him to that lonely street, assured himself of the man's innocence in the matter, then paid to have Erica and himself taken around the city.

After the second round, the weary driver pulled to the curb in front of the hotel.

"So," he said, "you have seen Lucerne. Twice."

"It's beautiful," Austin said.

"You have been to the Musegg Wall . . . twice."

"Very fortifying," Austin said.

"You have been to the Spreuer Bridge . . . and the water tower . . . twice."

"A fine work of engineering, but why anyone would want to build a water tower over a lake escapes me."

"To tell the truth, it escapes me too, and it always has. But you went there."

"Twice."

"And the Glacier Gardens. Now, nobody goes to the Glacier Gardens twice."

"Much too cold."

"Perhaps I can now take you someplace in particular?"

"No, I would like to see the city again. Let me be the first one to go to the Glacier Gardens three times."

The driver sighed deeply and threw the car into gear.

"Isn't Roger cooperating?" Austin asked Erica.

"I see flashes of things . . . images . . . but nothing I can put together. Nothing I can make any sense of. I see many things, but they come all together, like a badly edited movie. I see a man smiling. Water, blue water, the lake I suppose. I see a woman. . . ."

"Who is she?"

"I don't know," Erica sighed. "She comes and goes. Maybe she is a mermaid."

"They don't have mermaids in Lake Lucerne. Only trout."

"I see a funicular."

"A what?"

"A funicular. Surely you've ridden one."

"Perhaps. But I still don't know what it is."

"A cable railway. They're all over the hills around here."

"Oh."

"And I see a villa sometimes. A big house."

"A man, a woman, a villa and a . . . what did you call it?"

"A funicular."

"And one of those. Perhaps going up a hill to the villa?"

"I don't know."

"Perhaps the lady has a headache from so much driving," the driver suggested.

"She gets more out of it this way," Austin said.

Suddenly Erica's eyes opened wide and she smiled. "Seventeen, thirty-four, six," she said proudly.

"Hike."

"What?"

"Nothing. Go on."

"That's it," she frowned.

"Seventeen, thirty-four, six?"

78

"It's probably an address," she said.

"You wish me to take you there?" the driver asked hopefully.

"It'd help if we had the name of the street," Austin said.

Erica closed her eyes and thought. After a minute of this she shrugged.

"Seventeen, thirty-four, six," she said, "maybe it's a telephone number."

"You wish me to stop and call someone for you?" the driver asked.

"Any particular country?" Austin asked.

"Please, monsieur," the driver pleaded, "I am getting car sick."

"I don't know. Roger isn't helping."

"I wish this Roger would help me," the driver said.

"Back to the hotel," Austin said suddenly. "I know where it is."

"Where?" Erica asked.

"Back at the hotel."

The driver had the look of one beknighted. He spun the car into a tight U-turn and roared down the Alpen Strasse toward the lake. "Not since the Battle of Héricourt has someone wanted so badly to kill a Swiss," he said.

Austin was wearing a white dinner jacket. Erica Bergner wore a rather pleasant if conservative tweed suit. They stood in the hotel casino, sipping drinks, staring down at the roulette wheel, where the numbers seventeen, thirty-four, and six lay in a cluster.

"You're a genius," she said. "How did you figure that out?"

"Part of my checkered past."

"Roger played those three numbers every time he came here."

"The system of a man who doesn't know what a system is," Austin said. "Mine is much better. I worked it out on the NASA computer. However, it requires one thousand consecutive plays at the wheel, and I'm afraid we have neither the time nor the money to invest."

"Roger never won. Hardly ever."

"Let's see if we can figure out who did win over Roger. Why don't you scan the room and see if there's anyone you recognize."

Erica looked around the room, slowly and dutifully.

"Not yet."

"You're sure it was this casino he came to?"

"Oh, yes, all the time. Being right on the lake, it was convenient to the boat."

"What boat?"

"I don't know. That just slipped out."

"A big boat or a small boat?"

"A small one. I don't know, really."

"Well, that's something. Why don't you walk around. Mingle. Maybe a familiar face will pop up."

"All right," Erica said, and left for a slow stroll around the large room, which even at one o'clock on a weekday afternoon was filled with customers, some tourists, and some wealthy locals in formal dress.

Austin took his wallet from his jacket's inside pocket and peered in it. "What the hell," he mumbled, and sat down in the roulette table's only empty chair, next to a stunningly handsome woman in her late thirties. He pushed some bills toward the croupier and received a pile of markers.

"Fourteen," he said.

"You'll get more action by playing the field," a voice said.

Austin turned to the woman seated next to him and noted with some admiration a youthful figure and long, curly, honey-colored hair.

"I like to concentrate on one thing at a time," he said.

"You're an American."

"That's right."

"Then that explains it."

The croupier's voice was high-pitched, strident. *"Quinze ,"* he said, *"le quinze gagne."*

"I've known several Americans," the woman said. "They too could only concentrate on one thing at a time. So little imagination."

"That's hard to believe where you're concerned," Austin said.

Without her having to ask, a large stack of markers was placed in front of her.

"Have you been here before?" she asked.

"My first time."

"I come every night," she said, placing half the chips on zero.

"It's a way to pass the time," he said.

"Quatre. Le quatre gagne." The chips were gone. She placed the remaining ones on zero.

"You'd get more for your money using them as coasters," Austin said.

"When they're gone they will bring others." As she said it another large pile of markers materialized in front of her.

"My late husband left me a great deal of money, an impressive title, and an enormous villa . . . which is empty at the moment."

"Were this any other time, I'd offer to fill it for you. Where is this enormous villa, anyway?"

"Nearby. Across the lake and up the hill."

"Really? And how does one get across the lake and up the hill?"

"How do you think? By boat and cable car. My speedboat is right outside, in the lake."

"I didn't imagine it would be in the pool."

"You're so right. I am getting careless in my speech."

"It happens to all of us," Austin said. Then he picked up three of his markers and announced to the croupier, "Seventeen, thirty-four, six."

The woman's eyebrows furrowed. "Why do you play those three numbers?" she asked.

81

"I knew a man, that was his system. He played only those numbers."

"And this friend—did his system work?"

"Very well, for a while. He nearly won . . ." Austin shrugged, giving the impression that he was pulling a number down from the sky, ". . . a billion dollars."

The woman laughed. "He must have been an American," she said. "Americans think so much of money."

"And you don't?"

"I don't have to. I have a rich uncle."

"So!" Erica Bergner yelled. "I turn my back for five minutes and this is what happens! And on our *honeymoon*!" She slapped Austin across the face.

"Father was right," she said, "I should never have married you!" She wheeled around and stormed off.

"Excuse me," Austin said, pushing away from the table.

He hurried after her and found her waiting in the lobby.

"Next time try using a roll of nickels," he said.

"I had to talk to you," she said. "It was all I could think of."

"Well, now that you've gotten my attention, what do you want?"

"That woman. She's part of Roger's memory."

"I rather suspected it. Who is she?"

"I don't know, but she keeps cropping up. I saw a villa, a swimming pool, a patio on a mountain, I don't know."

"Go back to the room," Austin ordered. "Call Captain Sturmann at the Lucerne police and tell him Colonel Austin requested that a guard be put on you. Then call Oscar. He'll be at the hospital in Paris by now. Tell him I have been invited to another reception and have decided to attend."

"What if he asks me who this woman is?"

"Tell him somebody in her late thirties with a villa on the lake, a boat and a title."

"A title?"

"You know, royalty."

"The contessa," she said. "The Contessa de Arranjuez!"

"You're sure?"

"Positive. I saw her with Roger."

"I saw her with someone else."

"Really? who?"

"While flying to Paris from America I read a background report sent me from Washington. In January of this year she was escorted to a dinner for the Russian foreign minister in Paris."

"And who escorted her?"

"William Cameron."

"And the State Department knew this?"

"Of course. It was in a lot of the papers. And why not? Every diplomat takes a guest to receptions and dinners. It's considered bad form to go alone. Cameron's wife was dead, so . . ."

"So a minor figure in the Spanish royal family would hardly raise suspicion?"

"Hardly."

"Steve, I'll worry about you. I'm afraid it may be a trap."

"A trap? Of course it's a trap."

"But—"

"Now, I got home from the moon, didn't I? You make the calls I told you to and let me worry about being trapped."

Austin dropped the room key into Erica Bergner's hand.

"It seems I'm about to be picked up," he said, and walked back into the casino. The contessa was still in her seat and the seat next to it was still empty. With such a crowded room, that seemed an extraordinary coincidence. Austin pulled the chair back and sat down.

"Well, it seems my day is free after all," he said.

"I wouldn't want to ruin your marriage."

"Nothing lasts forever."

"Good. Then let us go to my villa and have dinner. I have some excellent wine."

She left the table without bothering to collect her remaining chips, took Austin by the arm, and led him out of the casino, through the lobby, and out the doors of the huge, old, elegant hotel.

Across Schweitzerhof Quai was a narrow park with two rows of well-cared-for trees, benches, and a short dock which jutted perhaps fifty feet into Lake Lucrene.

Tied to one side of the dock was a late-model speedboat perhaps twenty feet long. It was painted bright red with a white strip down the length of the waterline, and had what looked, from the size of the engine cover, to be considerable horsepower. The contessa stepped onto it, lifting her floor-length gown above her knees to do it.

"I don't see how you drove that boat here wearing that," Austin said.

"I had a man to drive me."

"I don't see him."

"And you won't. I just fired him. You can drive."

Austin shrugged, cast off the lines, and hopped into the driver's seat. The boat rocked back and forth with the force of his weight. She reached into her small purse, fished out a key, and handed it to him. He inserted it into the dashboard lock and a large Chrysler engine roared to life behind him.

"Where to?" he asked.

"Mattgrat," she said. "That point over there, east-southeast."

Austin kicked the gear shift into forward and the boat moved slowly away from the dock. When they were at a safe distance Austin pushed the throttle up to two thousand rpm and the small boat began to plane across Lake Lucerne like a flat stone skipping across the surface of a frog pond.

It was a beautiful afternoon, with brilliant sunlight that made the contrast between the white of the peaks, the brown and green of the slopes, and the blue of the water even more stunning than usual. A light breeze blew off the lake and up the slopes. Several excursion boats prowled the waters between Lucerne, Tribschen, and Lido, and in the cove off Stansstad two Flying Dutchmen were having a match-race. On their sails were the insignias of Switzerland and France. A score of rented skiffs drifted while fishermen sat idly on the placid water.

"I didn't get your name," Austin said.

"Luisa," the woman said. "Luisa de Arranjuez."

"That's Contessa de Arranjuez, isn't it?"

"How could you know that?"

"You said you had a title. I didn't figure you to be a duchess."

"You are a very observant man, Mr. . . ."

"Austin. Steve Austin."

"And do you also have a title, Mr. Austin?"

"Colonel."

"A military man! Funny, you didn't strike me that way. Army?"

"Air Force."

"Then why aren't you flying around someplace?"

"I'm on special assignment."

"To whom, or is that getting too . . . how do you say it . . . nosy?"

"Not at all. To the National Aeronautics and Space Administration. NASA."

"You are an astronaut?"

"I was. I'm sort of retired."

"Now I remember. You are the Colonel Austin who went to the moon. Am I right?"

"Perfectly."

"What do you do now?"

"Travel around giving talks. Lectures, you know. Let's say I put people to sleep."

"I understand. What brings you to Lucerne?"

"You forgot. My honeymoon."

"Yes, that's right. Your wife . . ."

"Erica."

85

"Erica seems like an emotional person."

"She has the emotions of two people."

"In my country that is not unusual."

"Is this your dock up ahead?"

"Yes."

Austin slowed the boat to twelve hundred rpm's and it dropped off its plane. Ahead was a two-boat custom dock, a wide stretch of wood with berths cut into the exact shape of the speedboat.

"This is it," she said. "Take the outer berth."

Austin eased the boat forward into its slot, doused the engines, and attached the lines. Then he helped the contessa to the dock and looked up the hill. A small, white cable railcar ran up a seventy-degree slope through several hundred yards of trees and bushes to a rocky ledge. Beyond it, Austin could just see the top of a large, old, white villa.

"Impressive," he said.

"I've always found it's what's inside that counts."

She drew him to her, brought his face down to hers, and kissed him. Then she took him by the arm and led him to the cable car.

"Thank you for rescuing me from another boring day with the same tired faces," she said. "You can't imagine how exciting it is to contemplate a fresh face."

CHAPTER EIGHT

The port of Le Havre is busy in the summer, because the Seine is busy in the summer. In addition to the low cargo boats and barges which can make it under the many low bridges, there are British Railways excursion boats, which ply the river as far up as Rouen, then turn around and go back to the sea. In that way the passport-less and money-shy may travel abroad without ever leaving the ship. At Rouen the first of the low Seine bridges is to be found. Travel further east along the Seine to Paris must be made by rail or car. The low cargo boats, so much like the colliers which ply the Thames from Wandsworth to Newcastle, and the barges, are the only commercial vessels capable of making the trip.

The Seine lets out into the English Channel a few miles east of Le Havre. The stretch of water between is a treacherous one. Like the mouths of many navigable rivers, there are wretched tidal rips and coastal currents, and shoals which shift location so rapidly that they make charts out-of-date by the time they are printed. So, in the last part of the century, the French dug a canal between Le Havre and Tancarville, a small village upstream of the mouth. Most of the traffic headed for the Seine first travels on the Tancarville Canal.

Mel Bristol stepped from a door marked HOMMES, wearing a fresh pair of pants and a new jacket. Still looking the part of an able-bodied seaman, he surveyed the port of Le Havre. Freighters, tankers, and barges were everywhere. Far from the pier another of the speedy British excursion boats hurried its scores of passengers up into the canal. Seagulls soared and dipped while others slept lazily atop buildings and dockposts. It was nearly dusk.

Bristol strolled to the water's edge, where a crane was busily transferring its load of crates from the freighter which had brought it from England to the deck of an inland barge.

"Monsieur," a nasty little voice called, "I must have a word with you."

Bristol turned slowly to see a customs inspector advancing upon him, angrily waving a clipboard. He was a small man and, Bristol thought, just the sort of diminutive civil servant who takes pride in keeping people waiting for hours for their passports, license plates, and inspection slips.

"We're almost ready to shove off, Inspector," Bristol said.

"Yes, and that is precisely the problem. I have not had an opportunity to inspect those crates."

"The papers are in order, aren't they?"

"That is not the point. We have certain procedures to follow. Regulations."

"Well, I apologize for the confusion," Bristol said, "but it's a rush order. We're due in Rouen in twenty hours . . . and we're racing a deadline."

"Exactly what kind of industrial equipment is this?" the inspector asked, growing more suspicious each second.

"Ball-bearings."

"Ball-bearings?"

"Yes, sir."

"Sixty-six crates of ball-bearings?"

"It's the biggest order we've ever had."

"Congratulations. But I cannot release them until I have had a visual inspection."

Bristal shrugged, reached into his briefcase, withdrew his wallet, and from it took a small card. He handed it to the inspector.

"If you'll just call this number," Bristol said, "I'm sure everything will be straightened out to your satisfaction."

With a dubious look the man took the card and strode quickly to the customs shed.

Bristol returned his gaze to the crane. It had finished its job and the tug's pilot was gesturing that it was time to leave. The sun was dropping below the Cherbourg Peninsula across the Baie de la Seine and the gulls were settling down for the night. Bristol checked his watch impatiently. Finally the customs inspector, his face ashen, came scurrying from the shed.

"Well?" Bristol asked with more than a trace of smugness in his voice.

"That number you gave me—it is *le président's* private line!"

"What did he say?"

"He said . . . for me to wish you and your ballbearings a safe journey!" The inspector scrawled his name along the bottom of a sheet of paper, ripped the paper from his clipboard, and, his fingers shaking, handed the sheet to Bristol.

"*Merci,*" Bristol said and walked briskly toward the tug.

It was early evening, still humid in Paris, and Oscar Goldman was irritable. He had missed lunch getting back from London, missed supper ducking reporters, and then was faced with another ignominy. He had to face the same reporters who were keeping him locked within the Hôpital Americain. Though there was nothing he could tell them, he was forced to tell it. Everybody was on him. Washington was on the phone every fifteen minutes, and the hospital administration every five. Goldman appeared to keep his cool, but those who knew him could see that his nerves were frayed.

Being a desk-bound administrator had been okay, as long as the projects were interesting and his side was winning. But now he was losing badly, and what made it worse was the feeling of impotence. He himself could do nothing but absorb the abuse of others: Washington, Peking, the reporters, and those in the hospital who were tiring of the whole matter. If he had to lose one, he preferred to be there in person, to have the satisfaction of having done battle himself. He wanted to be in Lucerne, especially following Erica's midday phone message. If there was to be another "reception," he wanted to be among the guests. The whole thing was maddening. Especially the reporters who crowded around him in the hospital lobby.

"There's really nothing new to report, gentlemen," he said. "Mr. Cameron is resting comfortably and his doctor is very pleased with his progress."

"Has the President spoken to him?" a British reporter queried.

"Not to my knowledge."

"Has he had any visitors?" a Frenchman asked.

"None that I can put my finger on."

"Why was an Air Force jet waiting at Orly Airport the night Cameron arrived here?" an American reporter asked.

"Ask the Air Force."

"They said to ask you," the man replied.

"No comment."

"Is there any truth to the rumor that the jet was supposed to take him to Red China?" a German asked.

"Where did you hear that?" Goldman snapped.

"Would you care to comment on it?"

"Absolutely not." Goldman turned and bulled his

way toward the elevator, the reporters keeping pace.

"If Secretary Cameron didn't go to China," the American asked, "where *did* he go?"

The elevator doors opened and Goldman stepped inside, flanked by two OSO agents.

"William Cameron is on the third floor of this hospital," Goldman said, "recovering from viral pneumonia."

The doors slammed shut.

"Vultures," Goldman mumbled.

"Mr. Goldman?"

"Yes."

"Dr. Wells would like a word with you. He says it's urgent."

"Did he say what it is?"

"No, sir."

"All right. We'll go to the lab. Any further word on this contessa?"

"When I left the operations room something was coming through."

"What?"

"I think it was the background you requested on her."

"Good," Goldman whispered. The elevator stopped on the third floor and Goldman strode down the hall to the laboratory.

"Rudy? What's up?"

"Oscar, you better look at this."

Goldman walked to where Dr. Wells was staring down into the maze. In the center of it a laboratory rat was crouching against one of the walls, shaking, apparently afraid of its shadow.

"What's the matter with it?"

Wells shook his head.

"I don't know," he said, "she's been like that for the past hour."

"They all look alike to me," Goldman said. "Which one is that?"

"The one that received the brain cells."

91

"How long has it been since it received them?"

"Eighteen hours."

"And how long has it been since Dr. Bergner received Ventriss's memory?"

"Twelve."

Goldman gave a small grunt in acknowledgment of the significance of that figure.

"Has anything like this ever happened before?" he asked.

"There are always side effects with any new experiment . . . but nothing this drastic."

"Then why this time?"

"Dr. Bergner's continually refining and adjusting the technique . . . but that doesn't necessarily mean it's been improved."

"Dr. Bergner's in charge of this project. Apparently she wasn't concerned."

"She believes in her work," Wells said. "She saw an opportunity to jump years of lab tests. I tried to convince her she needed those years to see where she was going and how much it would cost her to get there . . . especially in terms of higher forms of life."

"You're hardly the one to argue against unheard-of experiments, Rudy."

"You're mixing apples and oranges. I'm talking about Dr. Bergner. The mind is a lot more delicate —a lot more unknown—than an arm, a leg, or even an optic nerve. With Steve, all we did was provide the mind with new tools. Dr. Bergner was trying, in a way, to replace the mind itself. She was asking the original mind to step aside for a while and let another mind take over. The danger she runs is that the original mind won't like the idea. That is apparently what's happening."

"With this rat?"

"And quite possibly with Dr. Bergner. In six hours."

"What do you suggest?"

"Bring her back here for observation. A controlled environment where trained scientists can watch and evaluate what happens to her and take corrective measures if necessary."

Goldman thought for a moment. "Rudy," he said quietly, "the gold's cleared Le Havre, and we still haven't the vaguest idea how they intend to pick it up . . . or where they're keeping Cameron. Whatever information she can give Steve might make the difference. I can't pull the plug just because some rat's afraid of its shadow."

Goldman walked to the door, where the other two agents were waiting. "Let me know if there's any change."

Goldman hurried down the hallway to the operations room. There, his handful of agents and their telephones had been augmented with a Telex, a computer printout, and a stainless steel coffee urn borrowed from the Paris police.

"Tracy?"

"What?"

"Report. What's new?"

The agent shuffled through a deskful of papers until he found the ones he wanted.

"A man fitting the description of Roger Ventriss rented a helicopter from a charter firm at Orly. Ventriss paid for the helicopter in cash. It was rented in the name of a French pilot who was with Ventriss that night and who we are looking for at the moment. The reason given for renting the plane was executive commutation." The flight plan called for a hop from the Paris Heliport to a small town in the Maritime provinces. We have been there, and no helicopter came, went, or flew over.

"We have, however, confirmed that Ventriss was a regular at the casino in Lucerne. We have not established whom his acquaintances there might have been."

"And the woman?"

93

"Yes. We've been quite successful regarding her. The Contessa de Arranjuez . . . originally from Spain, Castille to be precise, distant cousins of the last Spanish monarch. She and her family fled Spain during the Civil War, taking up residence in the villa near Mattgrat. Her parents died years ago. Six years ago she was married to a Swiss national, one Conrad Steiner, a surgeon. He died of a heart attack a few years later. The contessa is a familiar figure in the casinos and restaurants of Lucerne, and occasionally roams around the Continent with jet-set friends. Her name crops up with some frequency in the French and Italian gossip magazines. Though she professes to be wealthy, it is thought that the opposite may be true. It's known that a year ago she accepted five hundred dollars to let *Vogue* magazine use her villa as background for a photo layout."

"Interesting," Goldman said.

"Isn't it? The desperate often do desperate things. Listen to this. January seventeen last the contessa was escorted to a reception in Paris for the Russian foreign minister. Her escort was William Cameron."

"That seals it," Goldman yelled, slamming the desk. "She's the key in this whole thing. She may even be the eyes and ears for the whole kidnap operation. Good work, Tracy. Now, get me three men, a briefcase phone, ask the French to give us appropriate arms, get a clearance from the Swiss, and, let's see . . ."

"Find out if the French have another of those planes," Tracy added.

"Right." Goldman's eyes were blazing like those of a foxhound moving in for the kill.

CHAPTER NINE

Steve Austin and the Contessa de Arranjuez sipped Benedictine from slender glasses as they walked along a dark hallway lighted by gas-fed torches.

"I trust you enjoyed dinner," she said.

"Tremendously."

"And that this tour of my home is not too boring."

"Not at all," he said, "but why does it keep reminding me of Dracula's castle?"

"Because it *is* Dracula's castle, in a sense."

"How is that?"

"The villa was built by a Berlin Jew who saw the writing on the wall very early . . . around the 1870s, just when Bismarck was making things unpleasant. He left Prussia and migrated to Switzerland, taking with him a great deal of money. He lived in various places, but then in the 1890s something inspired him to build this place. It's a duplicate of Castle Bran. Have you heard of it?"

"I'm not sure."

"Of course you have. It's one of the most famous landmarks in Romania."

"I'm afraid that country hasn't been in my itinerary of late."

"Castle Bran was built in the twelfth century.

95

Count Dracula spent some years in exile there, and when he built his own castle he modeled it after Castle Bran, to a degree at least. And when this man last century built the villa, he too modeled it after Castle Bran. Of course, the walls aren't as thick. It doesn't have as many fortifications. But it does have the high water tower, the inner courtyards, the exact same Gothic chapel. Why this man wanted to duplicate the chapel, I don't know. It has the same exterior. Looks sort of Tudor, doesn't it? And, of course, it has much the same sort of furnishings as one would expect in the palace of a thirteenth century Romanian prince. All sort of nasty and Germanic, you understand?"

"Where's the torture chamber?"

"I don't know. It's supposed to have one."

"Come on."

"No, really, Steve. It's true. At least that's what I heard. It's supposed to have a torture chamber and secret passage, just like Bran. I've been to Bran, and there the secret passage is near the well in the large inner court. Here, I can't find it. I poked around once, but couldn't find the entrance. Then I lost interest. One grows tired of secrets after a time."

"Have you no secrets?"

"Very few. I am a poor liar. Just like you."

"Am I lying?"

"You haven't said why you're really here."

"I seem to recall a little incident with my wife."

"Oh, Steve, I know that poor girl isn't your wife. I don't know who she is, but she's not someone you would spend the rest of your life with."

"Looks can be deceiving."

"Not to me. Come, let's go downstairs to the part of the villa I actually live in. This part is never used, except for official tours and state visits."

"Like those made by William Cameron?"

"Like those," she said, without flinching. "Bill is

96

© Lorillard 1974

King Size
or Deluxe 100's.

KENT

WITH
THE FAMOUS MICRONITE FILTER

DELUXE LENGTH

If you have
a taste for quality,
you'll like the taste
of Kent.

© Lorillard 1974

Try the crisp, clean taste of Kent Menthol 100's.

The only Menthol with the famous Micronite filter.

Menthol: 18 mg. "tar," 1.2 mg. nicotine; av. per cigarette, FTC Report Mar. '74.

such a dear man, I'm really quite fond of him. How is he?"

"I was hoping you could tell me."

"How should I know? I haven't seen him in months. Two, I think."

"Do you know where he is?"

"Paris, last time I heard. But why do you ask me? You are the one who works for your government, not I."

Austin and the contessa walked down a long, wide stone stairway to the second floor of the villa, where electric lighting was maintained and the musty walls were hidden by tapestries. A short way down the hall she pushed open a thick wooden door, then ushered Austin into her bedroom.

"I was hoping to ask Roger Ventriss where Cameron is," Austin said.

"Roger! Roger wouldn't know a *thing*. Roger is a little old lady. He can't even win at the tables, let alone be invited to meet someone like Bill Cameron. So Roger is the friend who told you about those three numbers on the roulette wheel. I was wondering how two people could be so stupid as to play that way."

"When was the last time you saw him?"

"Roger? Two, three weeks. He was just about to go overseas on business."

"Overseas?"

"To South America. Mexico. Some excavation or something."

"What line is Roger in?"

"Line? You mean what business? I thought you were a friend of his. He's a photographer, a *papparazzi*. Works out of his apartment in Rome."

"Probably the one place Oscar didn't check . . . Italy," Austin mumbled.

"What?"

"Nothing. Mind if I fix myself a drink?"

"Not at all, as long as you make one for me as well.

I would like a vodka and bitter lemon. There's some Schweppes in the little icebox beneath the bar."

Austin made two vodkas. The bedroom was a large one, with rather fading murals of long-dead maidens, a gold four-poster, an art nouveau cosmetic table, several large closets, and two French doors leading onto a large stone patio looking down on Lake Lucerne. The woman had left the bedroom and was standing at the rail, gazing idly across the lake toward the lights of Lucerne.

Austin walked to her side and handed her the drink.

"This is the most beautiful place in all the world," she said. "I have seen many places, but nothing to compare with this one. It has everything: the lake, the mountains, an ancient city. It has traditions, and it is new. I love it."

"You are right to."

"Now, tell me, why are you here?"

"To find William Cameron."

"Finally, the truth. But you will not find him here. He is in Paris. Or so I believe."

"And Roger Ventriss?"

"I told you, the last I heard he was going abroad. Why in the world do you want him? I remember you said: to find Bill Cameron. But two people further apart than Bill Cameron and Roger Ventriss you will not find. Why don't you go to Mexico and look for Roger there? All you will get is more bad gambling advice."

"No, thanks," Austin said. "Tell me, who were some of Roger's friends? His business acquaintances?"

"Everyone and no one I told you, he is a nobody. A little old lady. If you have to pick one of the two people to go and find, pick Cameron. He is heaps more interesting. And say hello from me when you see him. Honestly, Steve, I don't understand you at all. Either you are a madman or you are a much better liar than I thought."

"I'm sorry if I confused you with all the questions. Maybe I do have a screw loose."

"Well, I don't know what you want, but I know what *I* want." She tossed the glass idly over the railing. From the time it took to strike the rocks, Austin knew that they were at least three hundred yards up. The woman turned and walked into the bedroom. Austin leaned against the rail and watched her as she kicked off her shoes and reached behind for the zipper to her dress.

"Contessa . . ."

"My name is Luisa," she said, pulling the zipper all the way down. "If you promise to call me Luisa, I promise not to call you Colonel."

"Luisa . . ."

"Shut up."

She let the dress fall forward and slip from her arms.

"For God's sake . . ."

"Why are Americans always invoking deities?" she asked. "God has nothing to do with it. Get rid of your glass and come in here."

Austin shrugged, drained the glass, tossed it over his shoulder, and obeyed.

Bristol and the barge full of gold arrived in Tancarville just at the start of the tide, as per schedule. With a five-knot tide behind them to add to the tug's own seven-knot capability, Bristol found himself hurrying up the Seine at a good clip. For the first few minutes they rode behind *le mascaret,* the famous Seine tidal bore which leads the incoming water up the river twice each day. After two hours they steamed quietly past Villequier, the small village where Victor Hugo's daughter and her husband were drowned in a sailing accident in 1843. At Caudebec, one of the principal Seine port cities, the tug pulled in for refueling and rest. Bristol bought some sandwiches and a bottle of white Cote de Gién, a rather ordinary wine from Orleans, the closest thing he could find to a local wine. He sat on the afterdeck, ate, drank and watched the barge as the tug proceeded up the Seine.

The Seine is an old river and winds through a series of snakelike meanders on its way to the sea. It was in the early hours of the morning and a bright moon was shining. Bristol could see the outline of the ruins of the Abbey at Jumieges quite clearly, so clearly he wished for daylight and the time to sightsee. But daybreak brought only the city of Rouen, and a sharp buzzing sound from within his briefcase. Bristol opened the case, picked up the telephone, and pressed a button.

"Bristol."

"This is Oscar Goldman. Have you anything to report?"

"We are arriving in Rouen. The shipment is safe. We are five hours ahead of schedule."

"How did that happen?"

"A favorable tide and luck, I guess. Any new instructions?"

"Nothing yet? Anything out of the ordinary happen?"

"Just the looks I've been getting. I feel like Clark Kent. Every time I turn around I'm in a men's room changing clothes."

"Stay with it, Mel. We're getting down to the wire."

"Should I sit in Rouen and await further orders?"

"I guess you have to."

"I could use a nap."

"Take one," Goldman said, "but one thing, Mel."

"What?"

"Sleep on the crates."

Bristol laughed, hung up the phone, and closed the briefcase. The tug was pulling into the dock they had reserved in advance. Rouen is France's largest port, measured in tons of cargo, despite being 140 miles away from the coast. It's an industrial city, and as such suffered a great deal from air attacks during World War II, especially the Invasion of Normandy. One of the fleet British tourist boats was making ready to turn about and steam back down the Seine, its passengers full of stories on the bombings, how the churches survived, and on the burning of Joan of Arc in 1431 on the Place du Vieux-Marché. The last-mentioned event, Bristol thought, was the city's main contribution to humanity. The barge and tug safely tied up, Bristol found himself a cranny between two crates. He drained the bottle of wine, lay down, and fell asleep, resting quite comfortably atop one billion dollars in gold. Less than an hour later, a most extraordinary thing happened.

A young, female hand snaked slowly over Bristol's face. As the exhausted man lay sleeping, the young woman, moving ever so carefully, lowered a piece of wet gauze over his mouth and nose. Without being disturbed in the slightest, Mel Bristol lapsed into a sleep from which no amount of disturbance would rouse him. Her job done, the woman tossed the gauze into the river and stepped onto the dock.

"Very good, my dear," the chairman told her. "I trust Mr. Bristol will be quite placid for many hours."

The young woman nodded.

"Tell the men they may start."

The woman shouted a command in French and immediately a dozen men began untying the barge from its tug and from the dock. Into its place was moved an identical barge which had steamed down the river from Paris attached to the chairman's barge. This new barge carried sixty-six crates identical in almost every way to the ones atop which Bristol lay in drugged sleep.

"Make sure the men duplicate Mr. Bristol's sleeping nook," the chairman said. "I don't want him to —how do they say it?—blow the whistle any sooner than planned."

The girl directed the workmen as they placed several crates in a position identical to that on which Bristol lay. Then four men carried the American onto the new barge and laid him down in that spot. His briefcase and papers were moved with him. Soon the golden barge was tied securely behind the chairman's barge. The chairman and his secretary were having a quiet breakfast in the conference room, William Cameron was sleeping fitfully in his chamber nearby. Mel Bristol was asleep atop a worthless payload. And one billion dollars in gold was once again on the move . . . back down the Seine, toward the sea.

Three hours later Mel Bristol was awakened by the buzzing of the breifcase telephone. Further instructions had arrived from the abductors. He was to steam on to Paris, then to tie up at a newly vacated spot in the Port de Bercy. Grumbling and swearing, he shook the sleep from his head and went to find the tug's captain.

Dawn came to Lucerne as everything does there, spectacularly. By the time the first rays of sunlight were streaming in the window of the contessa's bedroom Austin had showered, shaved, and dressed. She was asleep in the bed, undisturbed by his early awakening.

Austin stood by the nightstand, quickly going through her things. Most of her personal belongings were unimportant, but in a drawer he found a large jewelry case. In it he found a passport.

He hurried through the rumpled pages until he found what he suspected he would find. He stuck the passport in his pocket and, with a last gaze at the sleeping contessa, walked quietly to the door. Austin opened it and slipped outside to find himself staring into the twin barrels of an ornate Ithaca-Perazzi MX8 over-and-under shotgun. Behind it stood Julian Peck. On each side of him was a guard holding a sidearm.

"I didn't know duck season had started yet," Austin said, closing the door behind him.

"You are a most extraordinary man, Colonel Austin," Peck said. "You can bend iron pipes, break through stone walls, and throw two hundred-pound men around like they were toys. I don't know *what* you are, but I intend to find out. However, I am right now willing to gamble that you cannot withstand two shotgun blasts in the stomach."

"I'll go along with that," Austin said.

"Good! Then there shall be no talk of escaping. See, we are both civilized men, capable of dealing on a civilized basis. You don't try to run off, and I won't shoot you. You tell me how you come to have such special abilities, and . . . we'll see what will happen. Anyway, I did let you complete your stay with Luisa."

"How thoughtful."

"Come along, Colonel. Let's go someplace where we can talk."

With Austin in the lead, the small group descended the main staircase and went into the library. It was a dark and unfriendly room, which, Austin suspected, was hardly ever used. There were floor-to-ceiling bookshelves, a large stone fireplace, and three great oak beams across the ceiling. At Peck's orders, Austin was roped to two of the beams, still standing, his arms apart.

"There. Now that I feel safe in your presence, Colonel, you can proceed to tell me what makes you so special."

"What's so special about me?"

"For example, how did you get through that stone wall in Kobá?"

"I kicked it down," Austin said, but in such an offhanded manner that there was little chance the men would believe him. Indeed, the two guards slipped their automatics into their holsters and exchanged smiles.

"You kicked it down," Peck said. "A four-inch-thick stone wall?"

"You asked, and I told you. Now, you tell me one. Where is William Cameron?"

"I don't know."

Austin sighed and looked scornful.

"Really, Colonel, I don't know. My plan called for him to be kept in a Parisian warehouse. However, the operation has been taken out of my hands, so . . . he could be anyplace."

"Who did the taking?"

"The chairman. You needn't bother asking his name. I don't know what it is. None of us do."

"Where was this chairman when you saw him last?"

"That is of no consequence. It is your turn to explain. How did you come by this great strength?"

"NASA rations. Lots of protein."

"Colonel Austin . . ."

"I don't know your name."

"Peck, Julian Peck."

"Mr. Peck, after you killed Roger where did you take Cameron?"

Peck's face whitened.

"How did you come by the information with which to make that statement?"

"Then you don't deny it?"

"No, I *do* deny it. I am just curious how you happen not only to be exceptionally strong, but very well informed. Informed with facts singularly lacking in decent evidence, perhaps, but informed nonetheless."

"If I told you, you wouldn't believe me."

"I haven't believed anything you've told me yet, Colonel, so why stop now?"

"I have only one more question, Mr. Peck, then I will answer all of yours. How deeply in this is Luisa?"

"Fractionally. She found out Cameron would be in that hospital, but has no idea what we did with the

104

information. I suspect she thinks poor Roger wanted to take the man's picture for one of his magazines. Get a scoop or something."

"And she doesn't know about Roger, either?"

"She doesn't know that Roger was a . . . casualty . . . of the Cameron operation, no."

"And the American ambassador to Mexico? Luisa was in Mexico a short time ago."

"She assisted in that operation," Peck said. "Now, Colonel Austin, back to you."

"Did Luisa bring me here so you could get at me?"

"Yes. Now, I saw you hang from the skid of a helicopter in full flight. How is that possible?"

"I have strong hands," Austin said dryly.

"So do lots of dockworkers."

"Look. It's just something that happened to me on the moon. Okay?"

"Colonel Austin," Peck said, storming to his feet, "I have about had it!"

"So, Mr. Peck," Austin said, "have I."

With that, Austin yanked hard with his bionic arm. The oak beam creaked menacingly, then groaned. A stone was dislodged from the point where one end of the beam was anchored in the wall. It clattered noisily to the floor. Plaster dust began to fall like fine snow. With an anguished roar the beam tore from its moorings and crashed downward, knocking one guard off his feet and forcing the other to dive across the room to escape death!

Austin then snapped the rope attached to his left arm and brought the bionic limb to play on the rope leading to the other timber. Peck, momentarily transfixed, reached for his shotgun, but it was buried beneath a pile of rubble. Stumbling over himself, Peck ran from the room shouting for more guards. Austin untied the rope from his right wrist, then pulled sharply on it. With a similar groan the second beam ripped from the ceiling! There was a deep rumble like that

105

which precedes an earthquake. The ceiling trembled and rained plaster upon the floor. Austin dove for the door and somersaulted out just as the library ceiling caved in, filling the room with four feet of stones, brick, plaster, and, most incongruously, the furnishings of an unused guestroom.

Peck was at the door, yelling for guards. He could hear the sounds of car doors slamming and men swearing in the yard. He scrambled to his feet. In the door to what recently had been the library were several building-stones which had fallen with the beams. Austin lifted one of the ten-inch cubes over his head and threw it at Peck. The man turned in time to see the stone hit the brick ledge over the front door and smash through it. He hurled himself into the yard just as the door came down on the spot where he had beeen standing!

Suddenly the villa seemed not an inconsequential novelty but the symbol of the enemy. Austin knew that if he had time he would surely level the place and sow its ashes with salt. But there was no time for that, at least not now. Revenge could come later. At the moment the only important thing was for Austin to escape back to Lucerne and have a chance to digest and analyze what he had learned. White-collar criminals get so chatty when they think they have the upper hand. Austin remembered that advice from an old Sherlock Holmes movie and, indeed, that day he had proven it true. Out in the yard, Peck was yelling at the guards to shoot the American on sight. Austin ran for the stairs.

He took the stairs three at a time and reached the second-floor balcony just as angry voices and shouts of "There he goes!" filled the villa. Austin ran down the hall to the contessa's door. He turned the knob, but it was locked. Cursing angrily, Austin leaned back and gave the door a vicious kick. The lock snapped with a high whine and the door slammed open, to the sound of one female scream.

The contessa was sitting on the bed, a sheet pulled up to her neck. Austin strode quickly to her side.

"You have one way to prevent me from killing you on the spot," he said. "Tell me, who is the chairman?"

"I . . . I don't know," she said. "Nobody knows who he really is."

"What do you call him when he phones?" Austin snapped.

"I never see or talk to him personally," she said. "I never met him at all."

The hall was filled with the sound of running men. "I'll be back," Austin said, and ran onto the balcony.

"Steve," she called, "it's straight down. You can't get away!"

"Rather late to be concerned about my health, isn't it?" he said. A guard was at the bedroom door. Austin held out his bionic arm, straightened the middle finger of his hand, and pointed it at the guard. There was a snap as the bionic finger clicked into place. With his thumb Austin touched a contact point hidden under the plastiskin. With a slight whoosh of CO_2 a needle dart shot from the tip of the bionic digit and smacked the guard in the eye. The man roared and writhed hideously, dropped to his knees, and within six seconds was dead. Two more guards appeared at the door. Austin's second shot hit one in the cheek and his third caught the other in the neck. Neither had the chance to use their weapons before the fast-acting, dissolving darts stopped their hearts. The dart gun was the only weapon Austin had which reached beyond his body. The revolving chamber still had three darts in it. He would save them for later.

Austin surveyed the possibilities of escaping downward, and decided that they were nil. The only way to go was up. He crouched, and then sprang straight up into the air, landing easily on the roof's edge, one floor above the patio. Austin ran to the front of the villa, where the third floor overlapped a second-floor roof. Austin jumped down to that roof, then ran across the top of the pseudoancient battlements until he stood directly over the door through which earlier he had tossed a building stone.

Peck had hauled himself off the ground and no doubt was in the villa, organizing the hunt. Austin had no idea how many more men Peck had, but he could hear voices. He dropped to the ground outside the door, and reached the cable car without being detected. He pressed the button for the dock and the car, an aluminum phone booth on a long string began its slow descent. Halfway down the slope, Austin decided he was home free and relaxed his guard. It was nearly a fatal mistake. As he began to daydream of the hotel and breakfast the window of the car blew inward from the force of a rifle bullet! Austin lost his balance and fell backwards, banging his head on the back of the car. He sat dazed for too many seconds as the car continued its descent. The window was gone and Austin was on the floor, his feet against the thin aluminum door. The car came to a smooth halt and Austin heard footsteps. A hand turned the doorknob. Austin kicked the door with both feet! It snapped off its hinges and caught the sniper full in the chest, knocking the breath out of the man. Austin flew from the car, leaped upon the man, wrenched the rifle away from him, and brought the butt down hard on the side of his head. There was a sickening crunch as the man's skull caved in. Austin threw away the rifle and stepped onto the dock. The key was still in the speedboat. Austin cast off the stern line and walked toward the bow.

"Hold it!" an angry male voice yelled.

Austin spun on his heels and faced land. A large

man in his forties wearing a black polo shirt had a rifle leveled at Austin's head.

"Hey, maybe we can talk about this," Austin said. He tried to walk casually toward the man but the man backed up.

"You don't look like the sort of fellow who would want to litter the lake with bodies," Austin said.

His only reply was the click of a safety being snapped off.

"Jesus," Austin breathed. He could jump left, he could jump right, but he had time to do neither! There was the loud report of a rifle being fired! The man's head snapped to one side, the rifle flew from his hands, and he fell on his side to the ground. Fifty yards away there was a rustling in the bushes.

"Oscar!" Austin yelled.

"Well, a moment in history," Oscar Goldman said. "For the first time, Steve Austin is glad to see me."

Austin ran up the dock and clasped Goldman by the shoulders. "What the hell are you doing here? I thought you were nurse-maiding the press in Paris. You look like a mountain climber."

"Today I *am* a mountain climber. It cost me half a hundred to buy these clothes. The gun is French."

"Well, *vive la France.* Let's get out of here." Austin ushered Goldman onto the boat, cast off the bow line, and pushed the craft away from the dock. A moment later they were skimming across the lake.

"I take it your departure was in haste," Goldman said.

"Something like that."

"Did you pick up anything of value in there?"

"A few fascinating items. How'd you get here?"

"To the lake? The same way you did. To the villa? There's a public cable car about three miles down the coast, with a parking lot and all that sort of luxury. I left a rented car there. You can drop me off. It's right"—Goldman pointed up the shoreline in the direction of Kehrsiten—"over there."

Austin spun the wheel and the speedboat made a slow turn to the left.

"The operation is run by a man known only as 'the chairman.' "

"Cute."

"Right. Very original. Nobody knows who he really is. In the cases of Scott and Cameron, the contessa de Arranjuez, whose charming replica of Dracula's castle just had its evaluation lowered by me, served as the eyes and ears. She sidled up to both of them, presented a soft shoulder to cry upon, and they cried. She informed the chairman, and one of his minions supervised the operation. In Cameron's case, she may not have known a kidnap was in the offing. Her immediate superior in the organization is one Julian Peck, who I make to be an American. It is his boys we are fleeing."

"How did you get all this?"

"Like the man said, there's nothing quite so chatty as a crook who thinks he has the upper hand."

"What man was that?"

"Sherlock Holmes. Peck said he doesn't know where they're holding Cameron. Apparently the chairman took him off Cameron and put him on me. Today was his second attempt."

"Three strikes and . . ."

". . . he's out. I think so. I think attempt number three will be the serious one."

"So we've got to keep you under wraps."

"We'll do nothing of the kind! Besides, I promised a certain lady in that house back there that I would return. Is this your cable car?" Austin slowed the boat to trolling speed and nudged the bow onto the grassy shore.

"I'll meet you at the hotel in fifteen minutes," Goldman said, climbing over the windscreen and hopping from the bow to the grass. "Try and get there in one piece."

"I'll do my best."

Austin shoved the gearshift into reverse and backed the boat off the shore. Then he put it in forward and roared across the lake. He had barely attained planing speed when he became aware of a similar boat maintaining an intersecting course.

Austin closed both eyes, then slowly reopened his left one. He concentrated on the zoom apparatus, and the tiny lens system zoomed to a magnification factor of fifteen. There were three men in the boat. Standing in the stern, carrying a sniper's rifle, was Julian Peck. Austin pushed the throttle as far forward as it would go. The speedometer read thirty-five knots. Still, Peck's boat was closing. And a boat on a plane is quite stable enough to be used as a shooting platform.

With a scream of shattered plastic the windscreen erupted from the force of a bullet impact! A second later another shell tore into the wooden hull! Austin spun the wheel to the right and the boat swung sharply toward Peck. When his boat was aimed so that it would meet Peck's, Austin left the wheel amidships and moved to the stern. This had the effect of raising the bow for use as a shield. Austin could steer crudely by shifting his weight from side to side. He picked up Goldman's French rifle and snapped off the safety. Then he stepped forward until the bow lowered enough for him to see over it.

Peck's boat was but a hundred feet away. Austin fired off three shots. The man at the wheel threw his hands into the air and fell over the side. The other man took his place. Peck dove for the floorboards. Austin dropped the rifle and grabbed the wheel just in time to avoid a collision! The small

111

runabout leaped clear of the water as it hit Peck's wake, slamming back onto the surface of the lake with a force that made the hull shiver. Peck regained his feet and a bullet shattered Austin's speedometer. Austin made a hard turn to port, putting the boat into a turn which nearly buried the rail, then aimed it for the second and final time at Peck's boat! Once again, the man was a hundred feet ahead. Austin rammed the throttle so far forward it nearly snapped. Peck was fifty feet away, directly off the bow. Austin made a running dive off the stern. As he disappeared under the chilly waters of Lake Lucerne he heard a deep rumble in the water. When he surfaced all that remained of the two boats was a ball of fire and some odd pieces of wood. He began to swim for Lido, a mile to the north.

Forty minutes later the desk clerk at the Hotel Schweitzerhof looked up when he heard a soft, squishing sound coming across the lobby toward him.

Austin's formal clothes were soaked completely. His hair was wet and his tie resembled thick seaweed. "Key, please," he said.

"Ah, yes," the clerk said dryly, "the bridal suite."

He got the key from its hook and slid it across the desk.

"I left my seaplane at the dock. I hope you don't mind."

"You have an airplane?"

"Actually I had it yesterday, when I checked in. But that was before I knew you had a dock."

"I see."

"Now you have two."

"Two seaplanes," the clerk asked, "or two Mr. Austins?"

"Both. Mr. Goldman and I are old friends."

"I see."

It was clear that he didn't. "Is Mrs. Austin upstairs?"

"I believe so."

"She missed a delightful swim," Austin said as he turned toward the elevator.

CHAPTER TEN

It was midmorning when Steve Austin let himself into the bridal suite. The entranceway light was still burning, but otherwise the white, false innocence of the rooms seemed empty. Austin kicked off his shoes, stripped off his jacket and shirt, and tossed them all into the bathtub. He walked into the bedroom. Erica Bergner's dress was slung over a chair. She lay in bed, wearing a plain, satin nightgown, the covers rumpled up at the foot of the bed, as if she'd had a restless night. Austin removed the remainder of his wet clothing, then toweled off and slipped into a fresh pair of pants. Erica was turning from side to side, moaning through a bad dream. Suddenly, with a scream, she sat up. Austin rushed to her side.

"Erica . . . it's all right." He pressed her face into his shoulder.

"Steve . . ." She clung to him desperately.

"Roger's memory again?"

"I saw him die. I saw the gun firing . . . it kept on firing. I saw Peck smiling. God, it was hideous."

"Julian Peck?"

"Yes, how did you know?"

"We met. It was charming."

"Peck killed Roger. Shot him . . . over and over.

115

I felt as though it were happening to me. I felt the bullets tear into me."

"You were reacting to what Roger saw and felt."

"No. It was more than that. It was *me*. I felt the same things. It was like . . . being shot to death and watching my own execution."

The woman was shaking, fighting back tears.

"It's all over now," Austin said.

"Is it?" she stammered. "Will it ever be over, completely gone? Or will I see that man . . . feel those bullets . . . for the rest of my life?"

"I don't know."

"You know what's really frightening, Steve . . . I don't know either."

Erica lay back and stared at the ceiling.

"Maybe you were right," she said introspectively, "maybe I went too far with this."

"You did it to save Cameron."

"I did it for myself. I did it to prove I could do it. You were right when you accused me of having that motive."

Austin took her hand and squeezed it gently. "Either way," he said, "I know what you're going through. Even if it's successful, it's not much fun being an experiment."

Erica smiled and closed her eyes.

"I hate to do this," Austin said, "but I'm afraid you're going to have to tell me more."

"I can't. Not now."

"Erica," Austin said firmly, "we have only sixteen hours in which to find William Cameron."

"Steve . . . I just can't."

She was interrupted by a loud buzzing noise. Once again she sat bolt upright. "What's that? she yelled.

"Just the doorbell. Lie down and relax, I'll see who it is."

Austin closed the bedroom door behind him and stepped cautiously to one side of the main door.

"Who is it?"

116

"Oscar."

Austin unbolted the door. Oscar Goldman still in his mountain-climbing gear, walked into the room.

"What took you so long?" Goldman asked.

"Julian Peck swung and missed at strike three."

"Are you okay?"

"Oh, I'm fine. But I'm afraid he won't be having anything to say."

"Damn. Oh well, we still have Roger and the contessa."

" 'Fraid not, Oscar."

"Why not?"

"Roger is out of commission. For a while at least."

"Then Rudy was right."

"What do you mean?"

"The third rat. The one which received the memory. Last night it began showing confusion, compulsive fright."

"You knew that and you didn't tell Erica?"

"Rudy wanted to. I vetoed the idea. Steve, we need her."

"Oscar, she's falling apart. I don't know if she can take any more. She's got to rest. Besides, the contessa said that nobody knew who the head of the organization is."

"Let me call Rudy. Is she out of earshot?"

"If you talk quietly."

Goldman picked up the phone and dialed a number in Paris. After a short time Rudy Wells answered.

"Dr. Wells."

"Rudy? Oscar. How is that rat doing?"

"Not well. It's still running around furtively."

"You'd think it would be tired by now."

"It's not physical, Oscar. It's mental. It's like an engine running at top speeed with no way to shut itself off. Eventually it burns itself out."

"We're talking about a rat, Doctor."

"We may be talking about a human being, unless somebody warns Dr. Bergner."

"What good will that do?"

"She can be prepared. You're willing to pay a billion dollars for William Cameron. Isn't Erica Bergner worth the price of a warning?"

"Yes, but no. We can't do it. At least not yet. Thanks, Rudy. I'll keep in touch." Goldman hung up the phone.

"What did he say?" Austin asked.

"The rat is still going downhill. He wants us to warn Erica."

"I think she knows already."

"Yes, apparently she does."

"Maybe I should tell her what Rudy said."

"No," Goldman said sternly. "Let her rest awhile. We still have one more avenue to drive down."

"What's that?"

"The contessa."

"I did promise to return."

"And you shall," Goldman said, "in one hour. But this time you won't be alone."

"You coming along? The old paratrooper returns to the battlefield?"

"I think I have already distinguished myself today," Goldman said stiffly. "I have three men plus Tracy. The Swiss have promised me half a dozen. I let them in on it. They're very sensitive about things which compromise Swiss neutrality."

"We'll go in by plane?"

"Plane and boat."

"I need two things."

"What's that?"

"A topographical map of the area on which the villa sits."

"You've got it. What else?"

"A Dracula expert."

"A *what*?"

"Don't argue. Oscar," Austin said. "We haven't got time. Don't you know there's a war on?"

William Henry Cameron felt an understandable sense of urgency, but he didn't show it. At that moment he was solidly whipping the chairman at chess. He had just captured the man's knight, announced a check, and watched while his abductor searched in vain for a way out. The search seemed interminable. Finally he could hold the traditional silence no longer.

"I hope everything is proceeding on schedule," he said.

The chairman nodded abstractedly, still studying the board.

"Then it won't be long before I'll have to find a new chess partner," Cameron said.

In answer the chairman slowly laid his king on its side. "Brilliant game," the man said.

"Why is it," Cameron asked, "that every time I ask about my release you manage to avoid the answer?"

The chairman rose.

"There are others who are also interested in purchasing your freedom," he said.

"And sweating information out of me?"

"Not everyone applauds your diplomatic daring, Mr. Cameron. When you flirt with the Chinese, you make the Russians jealous. When you smile at the Arabs, the Israelis frown. Each of your victories holds a potential defeat for someone."

Cameron advanced on the chairman with a deep-felt, almost pleading expression.

"I care about my work," he said. *"Passionately.* The world *can* reach an accommodation, an understanding . . . but it needs time . . . *I* need time to help it."

His plea was interrupted by the ubiquitous secretary, who opened the door and handed the chairman a note. He glanced at it briefly, excused himself, and left the room. As Cameron heard the bolt slip into place once again he turned angrily and with a sweeping gesture knocked the chess pieces across the room.

CHAPTER ELEVEN

The midafternoon sun shone down on Lake Lucerne like a white-hot diamond. On the short dock across the Quai Schweitzerhof, opposite the hotel, a group of men had finished loading arms and ammunition into the two seaplanes and a police boat. All the men save Steve Austin wore yellow, bulletproof assault vests. A highly pleasant, ten-knot breeze blew straight down the lake from Fluelen, following the River Reuss. Oblivious to the gathering of warriors on the dock, the usual flotilla of pleasure craft was out, and at Lido the beach was crowded with tanned men, women, and children.

"That's about it," Oscar Goldman said, checking his watch. "It is now one twenty-seven. At one forty-five there will be the fake chopper assault. As you know, the Swiss have lent us one of their CH-47C troop transport helicopters, which will buzz the villa, giving the guards the impression that an assault is in progress. That will draw guards away from the water. We will hit the coastline with two planes and the police boat. We will scale the hill and take the villa. When we begin the actual assault, the chopper will land five men on the roof of the villa, outflanking the guards. Any questions?"

"Yes," one of Goldman's agents said. "What about

Colonel Austin? He doesn't have a vest. Is he going in with us?"

"Colonel Austin doesn't need a vest. He has a plan of his own. I'm afraid I can't elaborate on it. Our best advice is to tread our own paths and let the colonel tread his. Okay? Let's go."

Austin, Goldman, and three OSO agents climbed aboard one of the French seaplanes. Tracy and four Swiss agents, including a pilot, climbed aboard the other. The Lucerne police launch held three men. If, as Goldman believed, the villa was the principal Swiss headquarters of the kidnapping ring, it was bound to be well fortified. There certainly has been no lack of manpower when Austin made his escape earlier in the day. Steve had accounted for a half dozen of them on his way out, but multimillion-dollar ransoms can pay for a lot of hired help. Yet if there was one person in the villa who could give them a tip which would lead to William Henry Cameron, the assault was worth the effort. The time was one-forty.

"I want you to take this," Goldman said, handing Austin a Smith & Wesson .357 Combat.

"I don't need a gun," Austin said.

"I appreciate that, but today you may need it. Besides, it's a good psychological advantage. Pull the trigger and that .357 will make a sound like the atom bomb going off, particularly in that old stone place."

"You pay the bills, you make the rules," Austin said, and tucked the revolver inside his belt.

The time was one forty-two. Austin fingered the ignition nervously as the sound of engines grew louder.

"That's the CH-47C," Goldman said. "Let's go."

On his signal the two Regentes started their engines and began to move across the surface of Lake Lucerne. The hotel faded behind until it was merely another building in what from the air still looked like a thirteenth-century fishing settlement.

The French seaplanes banked right upon take-off and rose swiftly to five thousand feet. Beneath

122

them the Swiss combat helicopter was bearing straight for the villa at Mattgrat, making enough noise to raise a hundred dead. To Austin's right Mount Pilatus rose nearly seven thousand feet in the air, a giant, snow-tipped cone in a sea of deep greens and browns. The planes passed over Stansstad, the bridge-line juncture between Lake Lucerne and the Alpnacher Sea, then banked left to follow a deep green valley up the road toward Stans.

The tiny village of Stans is dead center in one of Europe's great crossroads. Two valleys join there, one leading southeast toward Geneva, the other southeast toward the Grimsel Pass. Over Stans the planes made another left turn and followed one of the two intersecting valleys back toward Lake Lucerne, where they would emerge on the blind side of Mattgrat. As they skimmed the top of that mountain they could see that their plan was working perfectly. The giant helicopter, capable of carrying forty-four men for an armed assault, was indeed creating the impression that a full-scale operation was in effect. Several guards were scrambling up the hill from the dock to the villa, and around the villa itself other men were digging in and starting to fire. At Goldman's order the two planes ducked below the line of sight on the far side of Mattgrat, skimmed low over Lake Lucerne, made yet another sharp left, and skimmed to a landing near the unguarded dock. Austin cut the engine and let the pontoons edge slightly onto the shore.

The men hopped from the planes, ran up the pontoons, and jumped onto the shore. The sound of rifle fire came from the rocky ledge above and echoed across the lake and back again. Occasionally the staccato burst of the copter's automatic weapons could be heard. The handful of men aboard the Swiss chopper were doing a fine impersonation of a full airborne division, Austin thought.

Goldman announced that he and his men were going up the hill, using the cable-car ties as footholds.

123

Standing along the shoreline, half a score men from two countries checked equipment, recalled plans, jammed home clips, and switched off safeties.

"Your big moment, Oscar," Austin said.

"It's been a long time," Goldman replied. "Sometimes this business of working at a desk has it rewards. But there are other times—like today—when I would give away all the desks in the world for the chance to get my ass shot off."

"Let's hope it doesn't come to that."

"Worry about yourself," Goldman said, starting up the hill.

Austin watched Goldman as he and the other men began clambering up the ties of the funicular railroad. Then he turned and jogged along the narrow coast to a point precisely seventy-six paces from the southern property line. There, as plain as day, was a flue which served to carry runoff water from the rocky ledge, on which sat the villa, to the lake. The flue wasn't hidden, other than by a few vines which had the temerity to plant themselves around it. Flues are a necessity in mountain terrain, as a bulwark against manmade erosion. But if Austin's information was correct, this flue was more than normal.

He grabbed hold of the two-by-three-foot iron grating with his bionic hand, braced himself against the surrounding rocks, and pulled. The grate pulled easily from the ground. Austin reached his hand inside, then peered into the passage. His information, as he suspected, was correct. Behind the two-by-three grate was a passage four feet wide by six feet high.

After the contessa had told him that the villa was modeled after Dracula's castle, Austin checked with a professor whom Goldman had found at the university in Zurich. The villa at Mattgrat, it turned out, was well known in certain Swiss academic circles, perhaps better known there than it was by the contessa herself. The villa was not really patterned after Dracula's castle after all. It was a vague duplicate of a

124

fortified home built in the thirteenth century by the Teutonic knight Dietrich on the Hungarian-Romanian border. Castle Bran, as it was called, during the fourteenth century came into the hands of one John Hunyadi, a Hungarian prince who at one time gave shelter to a renegade Romanian prince named Vlad Tepes. Tepes, called by his people "Dracul," meaning "the devil," is credited with having executed some hundred thousand persons by impaling them on stakes. Thus was born the Dracula legend. And thus, was born the villa at Mattgrat, an approximation of John Hunyadi's fortification.

Austin knew from the plans filed when the villa was built in 1898 that it had an odd flue system leading from a center courtyard to a point just above the waterline of Lake Lucerne. This was apparently a nineteenth-century duplication of the secret passage through which Dietrich, Hunyadi, and all the other residents of Castle Bran hoped to escape their enemies, should their enemies happen to successfully storm the walls. Perhaps the man who built the villa in 1898 thought he would need it. Perhaps he wished only to be faithful to the plans of Castle Bran. Perhaps it was a joke. Whatever the initial idea, one thing was clear to Austin: A way out is also a way in.

Austin squeezed through the narrow exit and found himself in a long, straight, dark corridor. Walls, floor, and ceiling were made of polished stone. Bathed in the soft green glow from his bionic eye, the corridor looked like a tintype of medieval hell. Moss and lichens hung from many of the stones and a slippery brown algae coated the others. The floor was covered with six inches of slowly running water. High water marks on the walls indicated that during rainstorms the water in the conduit rose as high as three feet. Bending over as he ran, Austin jogged through the passage into the bowels of the mountain.

The cavern echoed Austin's watery footfalls as though they were breakers upon the beach. Here and

125

there a water rat ran squealing into a crevice. As Austin reached further into the rock of Mattgrat, the mosses decreased in density and finally stopped, replaced by the ubiquitous brown slime that was the only plant life capable of growing inside the tunnel. After a hundred yards the straight passage was replaced by a steep slope marked by steps, hewn from the same mountain rock as the tunnel. Between the steps and the wall ran a foot-wide water channel. The steps were dry, and the ceiling was high enough to allow Austin to stand upright. The stairs seemed to extend into eternity.

Austin began to run up the steps. Gradually the algae disappeared, replaced by dry stone and finally by dust and dirt. Fifty yards on there was a 180-degree turn, followed by more steps. As Austin reached the end of this second flight the sound of gunfire could be heard as a distant echo. Oscar Goldman was storming the villa from the outside. The fight was on. Austin ran down a straight passage leading to a huge oaken door, locked from the other side.

He pushed and pulled on it, with no luck. Then he stepped back a few paces and hurled himself against the door, striking it with his left shoulder, the one with the vitallium supports. The door fell straight forward, its old corroded hinges crumbling beneath the force of Austin's bionic blow. The door slammed to the stone floor with a great roar, sending clouds of dust to all corners of the chamber beyond. Coughing and covering his mouth and nose, Austin made his way into the room, a duplicate of a medieval torture chamber. There were no instruments of torture, other than a few ominous rings set in the wall, but the purpose was clear enough.

Across the room was another oak door, also locked on the other side. Austin dispatched that door as easily as the first, and found himself at the foot of a treachorously narrow, winding staircase which circled up a vertical shaft ten feet in diameter. Even with his bionic eye Austin could see no further than a dozen feet. He began a cautious ascent.

Austin could hear water dripping, but no water was in the stairwell. He could hear the sounds of battle quite clearly, but nowhere could he find a visible exit as he continued up the winding stairs, each step measuring one foot, until he had climbed over one hundred feet. A few more steps and he saw it—the stairs ended in a large stone slab set horizontally like a huge manhole. All along the walls roots projected from cracks between the stone bricks. He was just beneath the surface and most likely it was the surface oultined in the building plans. Castle Bran had a 150-foot-deep well adjacent to a similar shaft in which was built a winding staircase leading to a detention room and a tunnel to safety. The dripping water had to be from the well, just a few feet of brick and dirt to the side. The roots doubtlessly came from trees in the largest of the inner courtyards. Austin braced himself and pushed up on the slab blocking his exit. It was a good eight inches thick, but he did not have to break it, only move it. Austin made a gargantuan effort, straightening his spine and pushing entirely with his legs. The slab lifted slowly, then faster, dirt and small rocks pouring with the sunlight through the crack he was opening.

The slab tilted up to a dizzying angle, then fell over onto its side. Austin stepped into the daylight, squinting and rubbing his eyes. He looked at the slab and realized that atop it was built a stone bench similar to three other benches which ringed the picturesque well. The sound of gunfire was quite plain. Austin looked around. Across the well, seated on another bench, was a very defeated-looking Contessa de Arranjuez. Austin stared at her for a second, then stepped from the stairwell and walked to her, brushing the dirt from his clothes as he went. The contessa stared at him with wild, shocked eyes.

"Ambassador Scott sends his regards," Austin said. "He enjoyed your company in Mexico City."

"I believe we had dinner," she said. "Nothing more. I hardly remember him."

"Well, he remembers you . . . vividly. You're the last thing he saw before he was kidnapped . . . right outside your hotel."

"Unfortunate."

"Yes, but I'm more interested in your latest conquest."

"I thought that was you," the woman said, "until I woke up this morning to find my home being pulled down around me."

"I was speaking of William Cameron."

"You keep mentioning him. As I told you, he's a dear man, but he means little to me."

"He told you he was going into that hospital. You told Roger, and Roger had him abducted."

"Who told you that?"

"Roger."

"You spoke with Roger?" she said.

"He did most of the talking."

The contessa stood up and walked to the well. She sat on the edge and peered into its darkness.

"Then what do you want with me?" she asked.

"You can fill in some of the gaps."

The woman rose and faced Austin, suddenly defiant.

"With the exception of last night," she said, "I never give anything away."

Austin grabbed her wrist and squeezed it.

"But even that had a price, didn't it? How much did they pay you to set me up?"

"You're hurting me."

Austin let her go.

"I'm sorry," he said. "Sometimes I don't know my own strength."

The contessa rubbed her wrist, looking quite defeated once again.

128

"He said he just wanted to discourage you," she said.

"Peck?"

"Poor Julian. He's such a loser. He can't seem to do anything right."

"He caused enough trouble while he was messing up," Austin said. "Too bad he's dead. I wanted to have a few more words with him."

"Dead? Julian's not dead. Not unless it happened in the last hour."

"He wasn't killed in that boat crash?"

"No. Not at all. He swam ashore. In fact," she laughed, "he was convinced *you* were dead."

"I swim, too. Where is he now?"

"I don't know. He left here an hour ago. Why don't you go look for him?"

"Because I want to talk to you."

"I don't have anything more to say."

"I should think that you'd better. You're standing on thin ice as it is. Soon you will have nothing left to look forward to but your trial."

The woman sat back down on the bench.

"I suppose you're right. It's all falling down around me. You and your friends, they are shooting up my house. There is nothing left."

"Tell me about Cameron."

She laughed, a bitter, mocking laugh. "He told me," she said. "Like a little boy who just played a trick on his nanny. He was so proud . . . laughing about how he'd be in Peking without anyone knowing it."

"I don't think he's done much laughing in the last thirty-eight hours."

"I only passed along the information. I didn't know what they were going to do with it. That's the truth. Of course, I did sort of suspect that more was involved than Roger's taking his picture."

"What did they give you in return for this information?"

"What it takes to run this house. What it takes to

129

visit the casino every night. What it takes to be the Contessa de Arranjuez. I was lying to you. I am not rich. I have to do the best I can."

"And now," Austin said, "it's time for you to pay."

"How?"

"By doing something for our side for a change. I'm not saying it will get you off, but I'm sure the authorities will take it into consideration."

"Aren't you the authorities?"

"Me? I'm just a former astronaut, that's all."

"Yes, of course. You have your secret. Well, I understand so little about this whole matter, one more puzzle won't hurt me. What do you want me to do?"

"Sell out," Austin said. "And give us Julian Peck."

Before the woman could answer there was the sound of running and shouting from within the confines of the villa. A man wearing a harried expression ran down the west cloister and stuck his head through the door to the garden.

"We can't hold out much longer," the man yelled, breathless, before he saw Austin. When he saw the American the harried expression turned to one of horror and he made a move for his rifle. He barely had it off his shoulder when the garden exploded with the roar of a .357 Smith & Wesson Combat. The guard was blown off his feet, clutching frantically at his abdomen.

"Damned handy thing," Austin said, sticking the revolver back in his belt.

"A *gun*?" the contessa said incredulously. "How utterly ordinary. Julian gave me the impression you hurl thunderbolts."

"Nobody's perfect," Austin said. "You wait here. I have some housecleaning to do, then I'll be back."

The contessa nodded her assent. Austin walked to the cloister, stepped over the dead guard, and moved cautiously down the hallway.

The cloister led directly to the main hall, visible

130

behind two oak-and-glass swinging doors. Across the hall, Austin could see three men barricaded behind the front windows, hailing machine-gun fire on Goldman and his squad, who were pinned down near the upper terminus of the cable car. Austin pushed open the door and took careful aim at one of the men.

He squeezed the trigger and the hall roared with the magnum's detonation. The guard was hit in the back of the head and thrown straight forward, what remained of his head coming to rest on the windowsill. The other two guards wheeled and, without looking, opened fire.

A stream of bullets cut an arc through the ancient stonework and oak of the villa. Austin dove onto his belly and squeezed off another shot. He hit the second man in the shoulder. The impact spun him around, screaming in agony, his rifle clattering uselessly across the room. The other guard was delayed just long enough for Austin to fire a last shot. This hit the man in the forearm. The man dropped his gun and stared momentarily at his arm, hanging limply by his side. The man swore loudly, and with his good arm made a quick motion and clicked open a long stiletto. Austin threw aside the Smith & Wesson and got to his feet. The two men approached one another.

Charles Tracy, OSO, brushed the sweat from his brow and turned to Oscar Goldman. "Why do you think the shooting stopped?" he asked.

"Beats me," Goldman said.

"Want to make a rush?"

"No. Let's wait a minute."

"What the hell is going on in there? Think the men the chopper landed on the roof managed to get inside?"

"No," Goldman said.

"What, then?"

Suddenly the glass in the sole window which had

not been shattered by bullet fire burst outward as the body of a man came flying through it, backward and unconscious. The body hit the ground and lay there. Goldman and Tracy watched in silence for the most pregnant ten seconds they had ever known.

"What the hell do you call that?" Tracy asked.

"If I'm not mistaken," Goldman said, "you call it Steve Austin."

The figure of a man appeared in the doorway. "Come on in, Oscar," Austin called. "I bet you've never been in a Swiss villa before."

CHAPTER TWELVE

The Contessa de Arranjuez looked radiant. It was as though a great weight had been lifted from her shoulders. Ever since Roger Ventriss disappeared and Julian Peck became more in evidence, things had not been right. Then the American came and soon everything else was gone. She had to do something to clear the air, and she knew that the unusual American was her only hope for the chance to start over.

She sat at her customary table in the casino, putting her markers on zero, as she always did. All around her the early-evening crowd gambled and gamboled with no inkling of the serious business being conducted in their midst. It was a cool night and even in the casino she could feel a breeze blowing in from the lake. Suddenly, as if from nowhere, a man appeared next to her.

"You'd better have an awfully good reason for bringing me here," Julian Peck said.

The woman laid down her chips and looked up at the man coldly.

"I have something important to tell you, Julian."

"Well, what is it?"

"I've sold out."

She said it flatly, and Peck scrutinized her, trying

to decide whether to laugh at a joke or to flee. She didn't give him the chance to make up his mind.

"I've sold out to him," she said, nodding her head across the table at Steve Austin.

"Not necessarily the highest bidder," she said, "but certainly the most persuasive."

Peck stared at Austin with unmistakable fear.

"Julian Peck—Steve Austin," the woman said.

"Our paths have crossed several times," Austin said, "but this is the closest we've come." Behind Austin was a phalanx of Swiss police and OSO agents.

"I wish I could say I was sorry for this, Julian," the contessa said, "but even at your best you were a bore."

"Don't enjoy yourself too much," Peck snarled. "Mr. Austin is an American, and like most Americans, he will eventually go home."

"Not until I have William Cameron," Austin said.

"You'll have him as soon as we have the gold."

"I was thinking of a more personal trade . . . his freedom, for yours."

Peck smiled, almost enjoying the cat-and-mouse game in which he found himself.

"Are you planning to lock me in the basement of the Pentagon?" Peck asked.

"A French jail will do."

"Why would the French police be interested in me?"

"You killed a man there," Austin said. "They frown on that. It's one of those peculiarities of the French."

"And who did I kill?"

"Roger Ventriss."

Peck froze, his confidence gone.

"Roger is dead?" the contessa said, shocked.

"But the memory lingers on," Austin remarked.

"There's no way you can prove that," Peck countered.

"I have a witness, She can describe everything you did, everything you said, right down to the last detail. And when she does, that gold won't do you much good—at least not for the next fifteen or twenty years."

"There was no witness," Peck said.

Austin motioned to one side. "Erica," he said.

Erica Bergner stepped forward from behind the line of policemen. She looked pale, fragile, like a sick child. Austin took her by the arm and brought her face to face with Julian Peck. "Is this the man who killed Roger?" he asked.

Erica stared at Peck for a long, horrified moment as her brain turned from mere apprehension to a turmoil of fear, bullets, and blood. She saw his face smiling hideously as he pumped bullets into Roger. She saw Roger fall to the ground. She saw Roger bleed. She saw life escape him.

"I don't know her," Peck said.

"But she knows you."

Erica's face turned ghostly as all the blood drained from it.

"Erica?" Austin said.

Suddenly she lunged forward at Peck, her nails aimed for his eyes. "You killed Roger!" she yelled, then fell into Austin's arms as he stopped her. "You killed . . . me!" Then she was unconscious.

"Erica!" Austin shouted, staring helplessly at the woman. "She's passed out," Austin said then. "Find someplace where we can lie her down." Several OSO men cleared a spot on a leather couch and Austin carried Erica to it.

"Where's Peck?" Goldman suddenly asked. Austin looked around. In the confusion, the man had escaped.

"Stay with her," Austin told the contessa as he pushed his way toward the door. He ran from the casino through the hotel lobby to see Peck clambering into the driver's seat of his black Mercedes, parked down the block. Austin ran down the steps and

135

hit the sidewalk just as Peck gunned the engine and roared away from the curb, heading directly at the American. The lascivious grin which Peck wore while killing Roger Ventriss reappeared on his face as he drove the large car directly at the American who had caused him so much trouble.

Instead of running, Austin jumped into the road and began to run right at the car. At the last moment he hurled himself into the air, sailed over the hood, and hit the windshield hard with the soles of both feet. The windshield caved in like so much cellophane, and the car spun out of control, crossed the Quai Schweitzerhof, mounted the curb, smashed a cement bench, and came to rest against a large elm.

Austin extricated himself from his rather awkward position half in and half out of the windshield, rolled across the hood, got to his feet, and yanked open the driver's-side door. Ignoring the astonished crowd which had gathered, he dragged Julian Peck from the car and laid the unconscious man on the ground. All around him, people were jabbering in the plethora of dialects which substitute for a Swiss language. Austin stared at Peck for a moment, until his attention was distracted by a round, paper decal stuck to one corner of the shattered windshield. Austin ripped off the decal and the glass to which it was attached and stuck it in his pocket.

Three hours had passed. Erica Bergner was lying on the the great, white bed of the bridal suite, the sheets pulled up to her neck. Austin was pacing the floor between the bedroom door and the door to the hall, thinking about many things. In his hand was the piece of glass torn from the windshield of Peck's Mercedes. Austin was tossing it up and down absentmindedly, like Captain Queeg and his ball-bearings. There was an urgent knock at the door. Austin opened it to admit a drained and defeated Oscar Goldman.

"How is he?" Austin asked.

"Surrounded by lawyers. We could probably squeeze information out of him in a few days . . . Unfortunately, we only have a few *hours* . . . and Peck knows it."

"Where's the gold?"

"Just outside Paris. It will be in port in an hour. From there it's anybody's guess. Is Dr. Bergner awake?"

"She's been through enough, Oscar."

"She's still the only game in town. She's worth another play." Goldman strode to the bedroom door and knocked on it.

"Yes," came a quiet voice from within. Goldman pushed open the door. Erica Bergner was huddled under the covers, like the laboratory rat which was destined to burn itself out.

"What is it?" she asked.

"Nothing," Austin said, walking into the room. "Get some rest."

Goldman ignored him. "We still need your help, Erica."

"No," Austin said.

"I can handle it," the woman said, raising herself up on the pillows.

"I can't," Austin said. "I won't let her go through it again."

Still the OSO chief ignored Austin. He walked to one side of the bed and looked down at the woman.

"You're going to take William Cameron from the hospital, put him on a helicopter, and send him to . . ."

Erica closed her eyes, concentrating for all she was worth.

"Where is Cameron going?" Goldman asked.

"I can't see."

"It's down there somewhere. You've just got to dig it out."

"She sees pieces of things," Austin said. "That doesn't mean she can add them up."

137

"Steve, it's more than the money. It's a man's life. Erica, please try."

"I can't, Oscar," she said, shaking her head vacantly. "Not because I don't want to. There's nothing left of Roger. He's gone. It's a blank. Like an empty screen."

Goldman looked at the woman, his eyes betraying a touch of compassion.

"Burned out," he said quietly.

"I'm sorry," the woman said.

"Look, Oscar," Austin said, "we've been assuming that wherever they have Cameron, it's stationary; a building of some sort."

"It seems like a safe assumption. It would be too risky moving him around."

"Unless that's what it was meant to do." Austin handed Goldman the decal from Peck's car. Goldman squinted at it for a long moment.

"My French is a little rusty," he said. "What's that?"

"It's a pass to the Paris docks."

"The docks?"

"The Port de Bercy. Tht warehouse district between the Seine and the Garé de Lyon."

Suddenly Erica Bergner sat up in bed. "The ship!" she said.

"What ship?" Goldman asked.

"I kept seeing a ship. I didn't know what it meant."

"What type of ship?" Austin asked her.

"A ship. The type that carries cargo."

"A freighter?"

"Yes, a freighter! And another ship, too. The low ones. The flat ones."

"A barge?"

"Yes, yes! That's it! Roger remembers a barge and a freighter!"

Goldman and Austin exchanged strained, horrified looks.

"Does that mean something?" Erica asked.

138

"Not if that gold and Mel Bristol are still in each other's company," Goldman said.

"I don't understand."

"That means we go back to Paris," Austin said. "Can you make it?"

"Yes. I think so. No, I'm sure I can. I'm still a little unsteady on my feet, but it's over now."

"Roger is dead?" Austin asked.

"And buried," Erica replied. "I now know that in another six hours I will have lost all of his memory."

"And you no longer feel frightened?"

"No."

"Then it's over?"

"Yes, and my experiment is a failure."

"I would hardly say that," Austin commented, helping her from the bed. Already, Goldman was on the phone making arrangements.

"What will happen to the woman?" Erica asked.

"You mean the contessa? She'll go to jail, I suppose. If she can convince the authorities that she didn't know what the information she gathered was being used for then I doubt she'll be in jail long."

"I feel sorry for her."

"So do I," Austin said. "She's going to have one hell of a repair bill on that house."

"There are times when you can be quite heartless."

"Actually, a heart is one of the few things I can call my own."

"Sometimes I really have no idea at all what you're talking about," Erica said. "I think I shall go back to calling you Colonel. And just when I was coming to find you attractive."

"So you *are* feeling better."

"Much," she said sincerely, allowing herself to be drawn under Austin's arm, resting her head against his chest.

"I'm very grateful to you for seeing me through this. I only hope some good comes of it."

"Some already has," Austin said.

"What?" she asked quite innocently. Austin said nothing, but drew her to him and hugged her, tenderly and long.

Mel Bristol had a vicious hangover through most of the day, due both to lack of sleep and, he thought, the extraordinary potency of the wine. The hangover didn't abate until Amfreville-Poses, where Bristol took advantage of a tieup at the dock to dash into a grocery and emerge with bread, local sausage, and, miraculously, a six-pack of American beer. That settled things in his head, and he spent the rest of the day and all of the night stretched out on the afterdeck of the tug, watching his cargo and enjoying what was becoming an increasingly picturesque voyage. East of Rouen the river became narrower, less industrial, and more like a canal winding through old farmland. There was an endless array of bridges, most so low that Bristol often was tempted to duck. On more than one bridge he was able to pick off long strands of bright green vines and darker ivy simply by reaching for them.

The Seine once had a large number of hand-operated locks, part of the elaborate inland waterway system which allows travelers to visit most of Europe without ever setting foot on dry land. But after the war the Seine lock system was revamped, with many locks eliminated and all of them electrified. Still, at several of these Bristol encountered traffic jams which always disappeared magically when he presented the lock-master with the phone number of the President of the Republic of France. At some points he encountered war ruins which had never been repaired, but had been maintained as silent testimony to the deadly efficacy of American Flying Fortresses and British Lancasters. At other points he encountered different manifestations of odd French behavior, such as a group of islands near Limay where William the Conqueror died after being thrown from his horse in

1087. Four islands in a cluster are named Heaven, Purgatory, Hell, and Cheese. Apparently nobody remembered why.

It was nearly four o'clock in the morning when the tug hugged the right bank at Gennevilliers, then chose the right channel around the island of St. Denis. Halfway along the length of the island the tug turned right into the Canal St. Denis, a shortcut to Paris taken frequently by commercial vessels. By eliminating the famous Seine meanders Bristol would shave seventeen kilometers and a number of hours off his schedule. The canal was traversed quickly, until the tug and its barge reached the circular basin at La Villette. There, another right-hand turn brought Bristol into the Canal St. Martin, a remarkable stretch of water which runs, wide-open, down the middle of the street from Place Stalingrad to Place Republíque, in the center of Paris. On each side, Bristol watched as daybreak came to the myriad cafes, gardens, and markets which lined the canal. Bleary-eyed waiters took white, wrought-iron chairs from the tops of round tables and prepared for the start of another day.

At the Place Republíque the tug shut down its engines and was tethered to an electric tow car for the last leg of the journey down the canal. From Place Republíque to the juncture with the Seine, the canal runs in a tunnel under the Boulevard de la Bastille. When Bristol emerged from the tunnel he found himself once again in the Seine, at the Quai de la Rapee, less than half a mile from the Port de Bercy. It was seven in the morning when the tug, once again under its own power, eased to the long pier at the end of Rue Nicolai. On the dock, Oscar Goldman, Erica Bergner, and Steve Austin were waiting. The exchange of greetings and pleasantries was a short one.

"Have the crates been out of your sight at any time?" Goldman asked.

"Of course, on a number of occasions. However, the longest period of time was ten minutes. And you don't move sixty-six heavy crates in ten minutes."

"I suppose not. What about when you were sleeping?"

"I slept on the crates. I think my back is permanently injured."

"Doctors can work wonders these days," Goldman said. "Open one of the crates."

Reluctantly Bristol found a crowbar and worked it under the cover of the nearest crate.

"They couldn't have switched the crates," he protested. "It just isn't possible."

The cover popped open to reveal a boxful of gleaming golden bars.

"See?" Bristol said triumphantly. "Just as safe as if they were still in Fort Knox."

Goldman withdrew a penknife from his pocket and pulled open the blade. He hefted one of the gold bars and began to scrape at it with the knife. Beneath the gold plate was a blue-gray metal. Bristol's eyes were as big as the sun.

"Congratulations, Bristol," Goldman said, "you've succeeded in turning gold into lead."

"Lead?" Bristol said dully.

"Sixty-six crates of it." Goldman slapped the bar into Bristol's hand. The OSO agent stared at it with disbelief.

"I don't see how . . ."

"Neither do I," Goldman said, "but it happened. Do you care to amend your statement about not having let it out of your sight for more than ten minutes?"

"No."

"You're sure?"

"I'm positive."

"Then it happened while you were asleep," Austin said.

"Also impossible. I was only asleep for three hours. And I slept *on the crates.*"

142

"You could have been drugged," Austin suggested.

"How could I have been drugged without my being aware of it?"

"You fell asleep? It happened while you were asleep."

"It's not unheard of," Goldman said.

"But how could they unload sixty-six crates and replace them with phony ones in three hours? That's impossible."

Austin shrugged. "Only one way," he said. "They switched barges on you. They drugged you and moved you to a phony barge."

"Without my being aware of it?"

"As the man said . . ."

"Sherlock Holmes again?" Goldman asked.

Austin nodded. "When you have eliminated the impossibile, whatever remains, however improbable, must be the truth."

"One good thing about that scenario," Goldman said, "we know they're traveling by barge."

"Which means they're traveling exceedingly slow," Bristol said.

"Not necessarily," Austin cut in. "The switch took place at Rouen. If I remember my geography, downstream of Rouen the Seine is navigable to larger and faster boats."

"Yes, of course. I saw lots of freighters."

"Well, Roger saw a freighter too. I think they switched barges on you, then moved the gold to another part of the Rouen harbor, and at their leisure loaded it onto a freighter."

"Which would now be on its way to the sea," Goldman said. "It's the only way for them to go. A plane or train would be too conspicuous and too liable to detection. A barge would be too slow."

"How will they get the freighter through customs at Le Havre?" Bristol asked.

"How did you get through?" Austin asked.

"You know that."

"No, I don't. I was occupied elsewhere at the time."

"Oscar set me up with a priority phone number to give to customs. The President of the Republic."

"Jesus Christ, I think I understand," Goldman said.

"They'll turn it back on you," Austin said. "You came through customs flaunting the President, right?"

"Right."

"They'll go back out the same way. They'll say there was a change in plans. No customs inspector in the world is going to call the President twice. So they'll go through like VIPs."

"I feel slightly ill," Goldman said.

"Have you ever known a Frenchman to keep a secret?" Austin asked. "By the time they get to Le Havre that customs inspector you gave the President's phone number to no doubt will have spread the story all over the port. When they arrive, everybody in Le Havre customs will enjoy being part of the intrigue."

"And they'll sail right through with one billion dollars in gold," Bristol said.

"More than that," Austin said grimly. "They'll be taking William Cameron with them."

CHAPTER THIRTEEN

William Henry Cameron looked beaten, for the first time in his life. It had been several days since he'd last seen a razor or a fresh change of clothes. Such amenities were available on the freighter to which he, and the gold, had been transferred. Certainly, the chairman was always the epitome of neatness and good taste. Cameron's deprivation made him feel degraded, shamed, and beaten, like an aging alcoholic at the end of a binge. He had been at the very top, and now he was at the very bottom. He was becoming bitter; not even the richest and most powerful nation in the world had been able to rescue one of its highest officials from a handful of abductors. If such was the case, what hope was there for solving international problems, where the stakes were a good deal higher? Cameron was driven into periodic fits of depression by his captivity. Usually they were followed by temporary upswings of mood. He was in one of those upswings when the chairman came for a last visit.

"Your new hosts will be here shortly," the chairman said.

"Are you going to tell me who they are?"

"I think they would like to reserve that honor for themselves."

"What the hell do you think you're doing?" Cameron said, storming to his feet. "What gives you the right to tamper with international relations like this?"

"Ah, so there is still fight left in you. That is good. You will need it where you are going. The winters are cold and the workdays are long."

"I . . . could . . . do . . . good things," Cameron muttered.

"And no doubt you shall. You simply shall do good things for a different government from the one you previously served."

"This is more than criminal!"

"What is criminal, Mr. Cameron, is the fact that what I have done is considered criminal. We are all out for ourselves. In your former capacity it was your job to serve the interests of your country. It is my job to serve my interests. You flew from country to country, pitting one against the other, making grand and magnificent power plays, all to benefit your country. I do much the same thing, to benefit me and my staff. What is criminal, Mr. Cameron, is not that I do this. What is criminal is that my actions are considered wrong. Were I an elected official, I would doubtlessly be given a medal. Perhaps even made a president."

"I was working for the good of the world!"

"My dear man, I am not a schoolboy taking a citizenship course. Please do not treat me as one. Nobody is out for the good of the world. Everybody is out for their own good, be they an individual or a government. At the same time you preach the desirability of peace in the Middle East, your military draws up plans for the invasion of Arab lands for the purpose of obtaining oil. So, these are hypothetical plans, war games perhaps. They exist nonetheless. And they bear out what I have been saying."

"That is not true. I know of no such plans."

"Nor do I, but are you prepared to deny categorically that they exist? You have no reply? I did not think you would. You may have faulty logic, Mr.

146

Cameron, but at least you are not a liar."

Cameron sank onto the bed and buried his face in his hands.

"Do you despair so," the chairman said. "You will not be tortured. You will not be whipped. There will be no chains or shackles, no bamboo shoots under the fingernails. In time you will come around to co-operating with your new hosts. In time you will realize the truth of what I have been telling you."

"I am tired," Cameron said. "I am not prepared to ague with you. I am . . . tired, that's all."

"Soon you shall have ample opportunity to rest. You will find your new home a lot less hypocritical than your old one, and a good deal less frantic. A short flight by helicopter, and a pleasant cruise by submarine, and that will be all."

"I have nothing more to say to you," Cameron said. "From now on all you get is name, rank, and serial number."

"Ah! The warrior emerges! You are hardening yourself in your loyalty to your country. You will no longer listen to me. I suppose that is understandable. I shall leave you now. If it makes you feel any better, you are my last project. I am an old man, and now I am retiring."

"Retiring to where? There will be no place safe for you."

"Not true! I shall go to a place where there are people who also would like to increase their income. There, I will live out my years."

"You can go to hell," Cameron said.

"We are all warriors. That is where we are all going." With that, the chairman left the room, leaving Cameron to stare in solitude into his hands.

The flight down the Seine from Paris took a little over two hours. It was eleven in the morning of a perfect summer day when the French Regente sea-plane, which had seen more service in the previous twenty-four hours than most such special aircraft see in a year, touched down on the choppy waters of the Seine estuary off Tancarville. Austin brought the small plane to a perfect landing by the customs pier and held the plane in position while Goldman and Bristol secured lines to the dock.

The three men had barely managed to climb onto the pier when a confused-looking customs inspector ran up to them.

"Monsieur Bristol," the man said, "I do not understand what is going on."

"Join the club," Goldman replied.

"First the ball-bearings go in, and then a day later they go out again. Can you tell me what is the matter? I do not know what to believe."

"When did they go out?" Austin asked.

"Just a while ago. Fifteen minutes."

"What sort of ship?"

"The *Dover Queen.* She is here all the time. She comes and goes. Now she is gone."

"Where?"

"There," the man said, pointing out a speck on the horizon. "She is gone fifteen minutes."

"What's her hull speed?"

"Ten knots, more or less. She is an old freighter, just ten thousand tons. For years, she goes back and forth from Dover to Rouen."

"No wonder we couldn't find them," Goldman said. "They never stopped moving."

"Not a bad cover," Austin said. "A channel freighter moving with complete impunity beween England and France. Within it is the headquarters of the operation."

"You gentlemen are losing me," the inspector said.

"Up until now we have been losing ourselves," Austin said. "Tell me, where can I obtain a speedboat?"

"At Montebourgh. There is a naval station there. The *Dover Queen* appears to be steaming along the

Normandy peninsula, and she will pass Montebourgh before long."

"Can I land the plane there?"

"It would not be the first time Americans have landed there," the inspector said smugly. "I believe the last time you called it Utah Beach."

"I'm sorry. I was a bit young for that one," Austin said, clearly embarrassed.

"But if you want to overtake the freighter, you can take one of our boats. I can call them back by radio. They are still in our waters."

"No," Goldman said.

"Gentlemen, I do not understand this. I am afraid you will have to explain better than you have. I should like to know precisely what is going on."

"Okay," Goldman said. "Steve, take the plane and go after them. I will give you twenty minutes, after which a fleet alert will go out. If we don't hear from you in half an hour we'll board the damn thing. Take it right over."

"Fair enough."

"*Mon Dieu*," the inspector said, crossing himself. Bristol was quizzical. "Oscar, how can you send Colonel Austin out there by himself? I mean, one man against a boatload of armed men? They have to have a whole crew on that boat!"

Goldman put his arm around Bristol's shoulders. "What security level are you?" he asked.

"Five."

"Bristol, you're about to become a six. I have a few things to tell you about Steve Austin. First, let me speak alone with the inspector."

"Yes, sir."

"And, Bristol . . ."

"Yes?"

"Brace yourself."

"I need a hundred feet of quarter-inch line and a grapnel," Austin said.

"Of all the things I have heard today," the inspector

149

said, "that one is no problem." He ran off to the customs shed and returned a minute later with the equipment. Austin coiled the rope and grapnel and took it with him aboard the plane. Shortly thereafter, he was soaring above the water of the Seine estuary.

Three fourths of the earth's surface is covered with water, Austin thought, and the whole planet is covered with air. On the basis of those facts, it is not so unusual that he seemed to·spend a great deal of time flying or swimming. Yet it always surprised him to find himself so often occupied in these endeavors.

Austin flew low over the water, just a few hundred feet above it. It was his plan to give the impression of a seaplane pilot having trouble with his engines and on the verge of an emergency landing. The freighter was steaming along the northern coast of the Cherbourg peninsula, heading not for Dover but for the open sea. It was an old rust bucket, with streaks of corrosion leading down the hull from the gunwale to the waterline, and her cargo hoists thoroughly covered with rust. Hardly a luxury conveyance, Austin thought, but hardly could there be a more perfect cover. The *Dover Queen* was headed for God-knows-where, probably some banana republic with more greed than scruples, where the people behind the abduction could find protection. A billion dollars, plus whatever they might get from another nation for Cameron, can buy a lot of protection. Goldman was right. If he couldn't get Cameron out safely, then the Sixth Fleet would have to be brought in. No doubt this unknown "chairman" was armed not only with armament, but with papers identifying his vessel as the ship of his protector republic, turning any boarding attempt into an international incident. But they had started this small war, and now they would have to bear the consequences. There was a time when criminal action could be met only by immediate and deliberate action, regardless of whether it was strictly legal. That was the least the Americans could do for their foreign minister.

They owed it to Cameron. The *Dover Queen* was less than a mile ahead. Austin began to stall the plane, rocking it from side to side and causing the engine to falter noisily. The ploy had its desired effect. A half dozen men spread around the afterdeck stood watching the apparent disaster with mute seriousness.

The Regente skimmed past the freighter along its starboard side. A hundred yards in front of the ship, Austin cut the engine and flew right over the wavetops. He felt to see that his seatbelt was secure, then picked out a large wave. He gave the wheel a sudden shove forward, driving the forward tips of the pontoons deep into the wave. The plane shuddered and pitchpoled, tripping over its own pontoons, flipping tail over and smacking upside down onto the water off Utah Beach.

Moving quickly, Austin pulled open the seat belt, ripped off his shirt, and pushed open the door on the side of the plane opposite the ship. The entire deck crew was gathered along the starboard rail, watching the hapless aircraft. Austin tore off his shoes and reached for the plastiskin folds on the bottoms of his feet.

In addition to the components which actually worked his bionic limbs, Oscar had Rudy Wells build in an assortment of extra equipment. One such was the CO_2 dart gun in his left hand. Another was a tiny compressed-air tank with removable mouthpiece and face mask, built into a compartment in his right thigh. Simply lifting a self-sealing plastiskin fold gave him access to this equipment. Similar folds on the bottoms of each foot hid spring-loaded, foldaway woven metal swim fins. Austin flicked them open and locked them in place. With the line and grapnel slung around his neck, Austin dove into the water just as the small plane began to settle beneath the waves. The freighter was but two hundred feet off to port and, of course, was not stopping. His lungs filled with air, Austin dove to thirty feet and swam for the slow-moving

151

hull. His bionic legs gave him a thirty-five-knot capability under water, as fast as a porpoise. Within seconds Austin surfaced on the far side of the hull. Treading water, Austin uncoiled the line and, using his left hand, tossed the grapnel over the railing, some forty feet above the waterline. The galvanized iron hook made a loud clang when it caught the railing, a sound which went unheard aboard the craft. Austin scaled the line. Less than a minute and a half after ditching the Regente, Austin stood on the deck of the freighter. The boat was seven miles offshore. In twenty minutes to half an hour she would be in international waters.

Austin turned, flipped the grapnel into the sea and retracted the swim fins. In the distance, a group of party fishing boats were drifting idly off Utah Beach, where the American Fourth Infantry Division swept ashore just thirty years previously, shattering the German defenses with a loss of only 197 men. Austin's sightseeing nearly cost him his life. A guard, dressed in a black sweater and watch-cap, happened upon the American, slipped up behind him and expertly slipped the barrel of his rifle over Austin's head and across his neck!

Austin felt the cold, blue steel bite into his neck and fought for breath. Austin grabbed both ends of the rifle and pushed outward. With little difficulty he was able to push the rifle clear of his neck. He sucked in several gigantic breaths of air, then rejuvenated, drove his right elbow into the guard's stomach. The man doubled over with a yell, releasing his grip on the rifle! Austin wheeled and grabbed him with his bionic arm and flipped the helpless man over the rail. The guard caught his breath halfway to the water and let loose a blood-curdling scream. Austin could hear the sound of yelling and running coming from the opposite side of the freighter. He ran toward the bow and ducked behind the anchor winch just as a stream of bullets scattered off the deck around him.

The winch was an old electric one, its aging rust-

and-oil spots making quite a contrast to the shining stainless steel of the anchor cable. Austin reached along its port side to find the gearshift handle. With a good yank, he pulled the handle from its mounting, and found himself with a weapon. Then he found the pin which held the gearshift in the release position and twisted it off. The anchor flew to the muddy bottom, twenty fathoms below, and stuck there. The five-thousand-pound hunk of lead held the freighter fast in place. As soon as the several hundred feet of anchor cable had been played out the line went taut and the anchor dug into the bottom, causing the bow of the freighter to depress, then pivot around the anchor. The freighter was held fast by the bow, the anchor irretrievable. Seven miles from shore, the boat began making tight, desperate circles, like a broken toy auto. Everywhere men were running and shouting. Dead astern, a small helicopter was attempting to land on the deck. A number of the men, distracted by it, ran to greet it. Austin took the opportunity created by the diversion to hurl the four-foot gearshift handle at his nearest antagonist. The rusted steel javelin bisected the man's chest as if it were cutting butter! Eyes frozen open in stunned horror, the guard fell straight forward to the deck.

Austin ran amidships, bullets hailing around him. Deep inside the ship, William Henry Cameron listened to the gunfire with a mixture of hope and fear. Across the hall in a board room which was a duplicate of the one aboard the barge, the chairman and his secretary exchanged concerned glances. "Get me the captain on the phone," he said tersely.

Austin found the main companionway and ducked into it, two guards just a few seconds behind. Austin waited a half-dozen paces down the passage. When the guards poured into the door he charged them like a pro football back blitzing a weak line. The two men were thrown back onto the deck and against the rail. Austin dove his fist into the stomach of one,

153

then threw the crippled man to one side. The second was trying to bring his rifle into play. Austin grabbed the rifle and hurled it away. The Russian-made automatic soared over the bridge with a loud whine, dropping from sight on the far side of the ship. The guard stared at Austin in terror. Austin pointed to the sea.

"You can jump," he said, "or I can throw you."

The guard stared in shock for a second, then climbed over the rail and dropped into the water.

"They should all be so cooperative," Austin mused. He turned and ran into the companionway.

The chairman was staring intently at one of his favorite nondescript oils, in this case a rather oblique view of a windmill. A telephone was glued to his ear.

"What sort of assault?" he asked. "How many men?"

There was a long period during which the silence in the board room might have strangled a less resolute man. Quite obviously the captain was having some difficulty explaining the situation.

"Just one man?" the chairman said. "That's beginning to have a disturbingly familiar ring to it. Inform the pilot of the helicopter that he's still getting a passenger." He placed the phone on its hook.

"Unfortunately," he said, "not the one he came for."

He walked deliberately to the conference table, collected several folders, and shoveled them into a briefcase.

"What about me?" his secretary asked.

"I'm afraid there's only room for one," he said, patting her on the cheek. "Besides, your shorthand leaves a great deal to be desired." The chairman withdrew a nickel-colored Colt automatic from the briefcase and walked to the passageway door.

"If it's any consolation," he said, "I shall not leave Mr. Cameron in any condition to speak against you in court."

The small man stepped across the hall and fumbled in his pocket for the key to Cameron's door. A sound coming from the direction of the deck distracted him.

154

He turned to spot Steve Austin advancing on him. The chairman fired off three shots, but he was not a marksman—the bullets ripped uselessly into the wall. Undaunted, Austin kept coming. Frantic, the chairman ducked back into his office and slammed shut the steel door.

Steve Austin stopped by the door and stared at it. Then he turned his back and stared at the one across from it. He tried the handle and found it locked. He brought pressure to bear on the handle, but it only snapped off in his hand. Swearing quietly, Austin leaned back and gave the door a hard kick. The door whined and snapped open, crashing into the wall behind it with a great noise. Austin walked into the room. William Henry Cameron was standing by the bed, looking half frightened and half curious.

"Mr. Cameron?" Austin asked.

"Yes?"

"Oscar Goldman asked me to drop by and say hello."

The secretary of state gaped at the former astronaut, very much in disbelief.

"Excuse me for a moment, would you?" Austin said, turning to stare at the locked door across the way. Austin set himself like a mile runner at the starting line, then loped through the room and vaulted into the air, soaring through the open door and across the hall, feet first.

The soles of his feet struck the door with approximately the force of a medium-sized car striking a fixed object at a speed of forty-five miles per hour. The steel door buckled and flew inward, ripped from its fittings as if the whole thing were made of light plastic.

The girl was huddled in a far corner. The chairman was standing at the far end of the conference table, holding the automatic. A bullet whizzed by Austin's cheek and the interior of the ship roared with the report.

Austin dropped to the floor, and when he regained his feet he held the steel door in front of him. "That's a forty-five, I believe," Austin said. "Seven shots. You've used four. That leaves you with three." The chairman fired another shot and the bullet bounced off the door.

"Two," Austin said, walking toward the man, holding the door in front of him. Another shot rang out, and another bullet struck the door, sticking in the impromptu shield. "One," Austin said. He was walking blind, but knew that the man was right in front of him.

"Colonel Austin?" the chairman asked.

"What?"

"The ball-bearings are in the forward hold."

"Thanks," Austin said. He was at the end of the table. A last shot rang out but there was no ricochet. The girl screamed. Austin dropped the door. The chairman lay face down on the carpet, the back half of his head missing. Austin picked up the Colt and stared at it with revulsion. The girl was sobbing hysterically. Austin squeezed the automatic in his left hand and it crumpled into a pile of springs, levers, and twisted metal.

William Cameron was at Austin's side. Austin dropped the remains of the gun into his hand. The secretary of state gazed incredulously at the pile of junk.

"Tell Oscar Goldman you can drop in anytime," Cameron said.

CHAPTER FOURTEEN

Evening broke as it had each of the previous few nights outside the Hôpital Americain in Paris. Reporters and photographers jockeyed for position and insulted one another in a jumble of tongues. A fleet of Cadillac limousines, each bearing the flag of the American embassy, waited on the street. Erica Bergner looked radiant in a dark blue evening dress. Her hand was looped around Steve Austin's arm and she happily stroked the fabric of his tuxedo. Behind her, Rudy Wells looked forward to a quiet supper and perhaps a black Russian or two, his favorite patients securely in full health.

In front of the trio was a corridor made by OSO agents and Paris police and, on the other side of it, Oscar Goldman stood, surveying the scene with a commanding glance. A block down the Rue Chaveau, the Seine flowed idly past the Ile de la Grand Jatte, which did not at all resemble a large bowl, though it was named after one. Mel Bristol pushed his way through the crowd and handed Goldman a sheet of paper. Goldman read it, then walked over to Steve Austin.

"His name was Arthur Baxter," Goldman said. "He was a British national who was a member of the 5307th Composite Unit under Brigadier General

157

Merril operating behind Japanese lines in Burma."

"Burma?"

"That's right."

"Fascinating."

"There's more. Baxter was listed as missing and presumed dead following an assault in Araken on the border with India, February 4, 1944. Not a word since."

"And not a word after."

"Let's hope not."

Goldman folded the paper neatly in half and stuck it in his jacket's inside pocket. He pushed his way back across the corridor just as it caved in from the shoving of dozens of reporters. William Henry Cameron emerged from the hospital and moved slowly down the steps, surrounded by a cluster of aides. He looked in perfect health and was dressed elegantly. A thousand questions came his way, each drowning out the other.

"Gentlemen, please," Cameron said, "I'm still recovering."

"Can you characterize the treatment you received during your stay in the hospital?" a distinctly French voice asked.

"Let me just say that for the past two days I have felt like a prisoner." Cameron smiled and waved, then disappeared into one of the embassy cars.

Goldman was surveying the scene with commanding approval. An American reporter, a man whom Goldman recognized as an old hand at unraveling foreign intrigue, pushed his way up to the OSO chief. With the manner of a conspirator he took Goldman aside.

"I don't know how you pulled it off," he said.

Goldman gave a sly smile and glanced beyond the mash of people toward Steve Austin and Erica Bergner.

"Call it a miracle of modern science," he replied.

158

MORE EXCITING SCIENCE FICTION
FROM WARNER PAPERBACK LIBRARY